THE B[
ALMOST CO[

DIARY OF AN ALMOST COOL GIRL - 5 FUNNY BOOKS

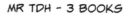

ALMOST COOL WITCH - 2 BOOKS   MR TDH - 3 BOOKS

DIARY OF AN ALMOST COOL BOY - HILARIOUS BOOKS
FOR BOTH GIRLS AND BOYS

KIDS LOVE OUR BOOKS!

Diary of an Almost Cool Girl

Books 1, 2, 3, 4

Bill Campbell

Table of Contents

Book 1

Meet Maddi – Ooops!

Dedication

Diary of an Almost Cool Girl is dedicated to the hundreds of "almost cool kids" I have taught over the years.

You are all very special! Don't ever let anyone tell you otherwise!

Thank you for giving me heaps of funny things to write about.

Almost Cool Kids Rock!

Where it all began…

The shrill sound of sirens vibrated the frame of the window I'm looking through. Up here on the second level of my school, I have a good view of the science block. Although the smoke haze is still lazily drifting from the smashed windows so the firemen could put their hoses in. Within a minute, they called out that the fire was under control.

I personally think the second fire unit and the two ambulances were a bit over the top. Nobody got hurt, and the fire was only in the waste paper basket.

I've been sitting in the Principal's office now for about 15 minutes, waiting for my mom to arrive so that the Principal can inform her about "How Madonna Bull tried to burn the school down."

They are his words – not mine.

How did I end up in the Principal's office, you ask? Well, let me explain, it's all in my diary.

Monday

Hi everyone, welcome to my diary. Some people write their diaries as private memories for themselves, me…I'm different, and I like to write it for an audience. My name is Madonna Bull, and most people call me Maddi.

Some kids call me Mad or even Mad Bull, but I just ignore those types of kids. I'm not one of the "cool" kids, and I'm not one of the "brainy" kids…I'm just a normal girl. Sometimes I like to think of myself as an "almost cool girl." Not in the "cool" group, but I'm not a nerd either.

I'm 12, well, nearly 12. Okay, I'm 11 years, six months, and three days to be exact.

I must confess, I have a bad habit. I like to give people nicknames, but don't panic. I don't call anyone by their nicknames, and I just use them in my diary. So, I guess only you and I know about them.

For example, my mom is an alternative hippy type mom, carefree, and always looking on the bright side of things. Like when I dropped two dinner plates, and they both broke, Mom comes out with, "That's okay, Madonna, it just means less washing up to do."

And that is why her nickname is Mrs. Absolutely Positive. She is positive and enthusiastic about EVERYTHING! Mom also loves exercise, yoga, and healthy food. She is really into those yucky green drinks with vegetables in them…gross!

Dad is big with a loud booming voice, so his nickname is Mr. Boom Boom. I wonder what my nickname for you would be if I knew you.

I blame my parents for the "nickname" thing. They give everyone in our neighborhood a nickname. Sometimes it is a bit embarrassing because we don't remember their real names. Labrador man (yes, he walks a Labrador dog) and Bob (not his real name, but he is a builder – like Bob The Builder) all live close by. So, using nicknames is a family tradition that I have inherited.

My parents have given me some shocking nicknames. The

first one was Poo Shooter. When I was a baby, my superpower was to shoot explosive poos across the room.

When I got a bit older, around 6, they called me Princess Grotty Snotty due to an unfortunate incident when I was wearing my best princess costume. I had a cold, and my nose was full of thick gooey green snot.

Mom had taken me to the shopping center to go to the doctors, and on the way out, we took a shortcut through the food court. That's where it all went terribly wrong.

Halfway through the eating area, a dear old granny-type lady said to my mom, "What a beautiful princess you have there" – that's me, of course.

Granny lady stops eating her lovely-looking cake and starts telling me how pretty I look. You know how, when you have a cold, you have no control over when your body decides to sneeze…well, my body decided to sneeze just as she finished those kind words and smiled at me. Not just any sneeze, but perhaps the biggest and greatest sneeze in the history of mankind. Ahhhhh Chooooo!!!!

That stopped the granny lady in her tracks. She looked down at her yummy cake, and it is covered in two rivers of snot. She claps her hands across her mouth. Making retching sounds, she races from her table towards the toilets.

Meanwhile, mom grabs my hand and drags me off to the car. Being Mrs. AbsolutelyPositive, she says, "It's okay, Maddi, better out than in. And besides, that cake was so unhealthy. She would have been much better off eating some nice fresh fruit." Did I mention that Mom is really into healthy food?

And that is how I collected the lovely nickname of Princess Grotty Snotty.

Anyway, enough diary for today, I need to do my homework and so probably do you.

Tuesday

My best friend Shelby and I walked to school this morning. We have been friends for a long time now, since about halfway through last year. I'm pretty quiet and try to avoid being the center of attention, while Shelby is the opposite. She is loud and outgoing and loves being in the spotlight.

Mom says we get along so well because we balance each other out. She said something about yin and yang, but I have no idea what she is talking about.

Today when we were in Music class, we were sitting together as always. Mr. Canary (not his real name, just a great nickname, loves to sing his instructions to us) asked us to sit on the floor in a circle.

Mr. Canary clapped out a rhythmic pattern, and we each, in turn, had to copy his pattern. Of course, the pattern changed for each student.

Music is not my strong point. Even when trying to clap the beat to a song, I'm likely to miss my own hands altogether. Obviously, I'm not the only one feeling the pressure…as everyone is absolutely quiet as we await our turns.

There is a pause after each time Mr. Canary demonstrates a clapping pattern, and in those few seconds, you could hear a pin drop. It's nearly our turn; I can see Shelby is nervous as she keeps fidgeting.

I'm so glad she is before me as it gives me a little more time. If you get the clapping pattern correct, Mr. Canary gives you a treat. So, as well as not wanting to embarrass myself, I also really want a treat!

Mr. Canary claps out the rhythm for the girl sitting next to Shelby, and the silence before the girl starts her turn seems absolute. Until an eardrum-bursting fart noise rips across the room, I can even feel the vibration on the wooden floor and instantly realize that Shelby is the source of the noise. Poor Shelby! I feel embarrassed for her, so I try to think of something to say to ease her embarrassment.

No need – Shelby's next comment solves the problem. "Oh, Maddi, that smells terrible!"

"I'm sorry, Sir, Maddi has been suffering diarrhea. I'll just take her to the toilet and make sure she is okay." Then Shelby rustles me out of the classroom door as the laughter from the rest of the class drowns out my protests of innocence.

Once outside, Shelby breaks into hysterical laughter, humiliating me even more.

But in the end, I give up and join in the laughter. Eventually, Shelby says, "Well, Maddi, I may have ruined your image, but at least I got us out of clapping those stupid patterns."

Thursday

Despite the odd embarrassing moment, I'm lucky to have a good friend like Shelby. Having friends is especially important when you have a Bethany Barker in your class. Bethany is the mean girl at our school. Some kids love sport, some love achieving A's, some love the arts, but Bethany just loves being mean. That's right, folks, a genuine bully in my class.

Generally, I don't have too much trouble with her. Shelby and I are nearly always together, and Shelby is simply too loud to pick on. I've already told Bethany – whom I secretly call MG (short for a mean girl), that I don't really care about her opinion.

One day MG must have been low on her quota of kids to pick on when she came across Shelby and me in the playground. MG started making negative and nasty comments about my appearance. Like all bullies, MG always seemed to have a little band of followers. Sarah and Sue (who must be very desperate for friends to hang out with MG) were with MG. As usual, MG would make nasty remarks, and her followers, Sarah and Sue, would laugh at her "amazing" wit.

Mom always taught me the best way to deal with bullies is to ignore them or stand up to them. I decided to try a bit of both. First, I just totally ignored MG's nasty comments, and I kept talking to Shelby.

After about 5 minutes of ignoring MG's little rant, I saw Shelby's face begin to show her anger at her friend being insulted.

I put my hand softly on her shoulder and said, "It's okay; I'll handle this."

I turned to MG and calmly said, "Thanks to Bethany, I'm always ready to accept constructive criticism about my appearance from intelligent, fashionable, and thoughtful people like yourself."
Bethany looked confused.

Then I continued in a calm and confident voice, "But hang on, I just realized you're definitely not intelligent, nor thoughtful, and perhaps not even fashionable, so I really couldn't care less about your opinion."

Shelby burst into laughter. Even one of MG's cronies had a little chuckle.

I led Shelby away as MG growled at her friends for laughing.

Friday

Today during the lunch break, MG was picking on Caroline. Caroline is only new to my school and tends to keep to herself. At first, we didn't realize what was happening, but as soon as we did, Shelby and I sat on either side of her.

"Bye Bethany," says Shelby in her best "I'm not scared of you" tone of voice. Ever since our last run-in with Bethany, she has avoided us – which we love! Bethany shrugs her shoulders, pokes her tongue out, and stomps off in a huff.

That's when we see the tears in Caroline's eyes. She reveals that MG has been bullying her almost every day since she arrived at our school. MG has been quietly calling her names in class. So quiet that the teacher and other kids can't hear. And she has been pushing her books off the table as she walks past Caroline's desk.

We tell Caroline that she should tell the teacher what is happening, but apparently, MG told Caroline that the teachers at our school hate kids who tell on other kids and that the teachers will only tell her to "just deal with it."

Shelby and I are horrified. I explain to Caroline that bullies often make up stories like this to stop their victims from getting help. "Our teachers are great! If you tell them about Bethany, they'll do their best to stop her," I explained.

Monday

In the morning, Caroline told us that she had taken our advice and spoken to her favorite teacher, Miss Jenkins. At about 9:30, the principal came into the classroom and took Caroline away for about an hour.

Then when he returned with Caroline, he took MG away with him. She walked back into the classroom about 40 minutes later. MG's shoulders were slumped as she quietly returned to her seat. It looked like she had been crying.

At the first break, MG kept well away from Caroline. She sat and ate her apple and didn't strut around looking for victims like she does every other break.

Caroline told us that the principal (I call him Mr. Sausage Nose – he has a long nose) wanted to know everything that MG had done. She said he was great, and he assured her that he would speak to Bethany and that Caroline should come directly to him if she bothered her anymore. Caroline was so happy and couldn't stop thanking us for giving her the courage to speak up. Hi-5's all around.

Bullies 0 – Almost Cool Girls 1!

Tuesday

Mathematics today was so boring! Mr. Wettan, or as I like to call him, Mr. Facebook…was at his worst. Unfortunately, I have him for both Math and Science, so he is double trouble and doubly bad!

Mr. Facebook (can you guess why?) is only a young teacher. He always has his phone on his desk with Facebook open.

Today he started with a lesson on fractions, and this lesson was beginning to look interesting when his phone made a quiet ding sound. You know the type of noise that lets you know when someone has posted something on your wall. Mid-sentence, Mr. Facebook stops talking and rushes over to his phone. He has a quiet chuckle to himself and suddenly realizes the whole class is sitting there watching him.

He quickly brings up a Math video on the data projector and instructs us to watch it. Then he sits at his desk and taps out messages on his phone for the rest of the lesson. The video was boring! The best part was when the principal walked in. Mr. Facebook jumped out of his chair like a startled rabbit! That phone disappeared so fast into his pocket that he may have set a new "hide the phone, speed record."

I think the principal may have seen it. They had a short conversation, and although I couldn't make out the words, the tone of voice from the principal didn't sound very happy. When the principal left, the phone stayed in Mr. Facebook's pocket. It was funny because every couple of minutes, we could see it vibrating.

Wednesday

The day I've been dreading has finally arrived. I did my best to avoid it! I tried to hide those notes at the bottom of my school bag. I deleted those online school newsletters as soon as I could from our home computer. I even tried to fake being too sick to go to school today, but all that got me was a big spoon of apple cider vinegar. Yuck!!!!! Seriously…do normal kids with normal parents have to gulp down that foul-tasting vinegar? Uugghh! I'm sure that one day it will turn me into a full-blown zombie!

Sadly, all my best efforts have failed, and today Mom is coming to school with me. She is volunteering in the school canteen for a day.

Now I love my Mom…it's just when it comes to food, she is VERY alternative. We eat enough salads to feed the vast grazing herds of Africa! Mom's idea of junk food is dipping your carrot stick into yogurt. If it weren't for Dad, I wouldn't even know about sugar or chocolate.

Our school canteen sells what they call a balanced menu. That means some healthy foods (by normal standards) and some less healthy foods – the yummy stuff. I'm a bit worried about how Mom will cope with serving up food that goes against her healthy food values.

Once at school, Mom puts on her school canteen apron and bids me goodbye, with a cheery, "Be the best you can be, Madonna." That's my Mom, Mrs. Absolutely Positive.

I should have realized something was wrong when I kept getting odd looks as some of my classmates arrived in our room after putting in their canteen orders.

Lunchtime revealed the full extent of my problem when a group of about ten students approached me as I sat next to Shelby, and we began eating our lunch. Tiny (my nickname for David Burrows – the class football hero – who was actually a giant!) stood in front of me. "Maddi, is that your mother in the canteen? The one who is ruining all our lunches!"

"Well," I mumbled, "my mom is in the canteen; she is quite a good cook. I don't think she would RUIN anyone's lunch."

Then the whole group started yelling out their complaints in a storm of jumbled words.

"She made me have brown bread!"

"My ham and salad roll had NO ham!"

"My hotdog had tofu instead of a sausage!"

"I ordered a bag of chips, and I got carrot and celery sticks!"

"She scraped all the icing off my cake and said there was enough sugar in the cake!"

"And I wanted a chocolate milkshake, and she gave me a green smoothie, gross!!!! It looked like snot!"

This required some quick thinking! I smiled, "Well, the good news is that you are all looking a lot healthier, and Mom is only working in the canteen once a week for the rest of the term."

All the junk and fatty food fans started groaning, and Shelby and I quickly made out escape towards the playground.

I didn't even bother discussing the canteen complaints with my mother that night. I know what her response would be, and I don't feel like a food lecture.

Besides, I have to eat healthy food every day…it won't hurt them to have it once a week!

Saturday

What a day! Mom had invited her friend Demi over for lunch. Demi is an artist, and while Mom is a bit of a hippy, Demi is an extreme "free spirit" type of person. Her daughter's name is Star, and she is a year older than me. Star doesn't go to school; she is home-schooled. Don't get me wrong, I have nothing against homeschooling, in fact, I think homeschooling would be great, but I think Star's education would be very different from my school. Math would probably involve a visit to the local hippy store and adding up the prices of all the weirdo hats. History would probably be watching an old movie. And Science would be gazing at the stars when night falls. Actually, it sounds pretty good!

Anyway, I discovered Demi and mom talking in the kitchen as they prepared lunch. Demi greeted me with a cheery, "Hi Maddi, wow, your aura is looking so bright and happy." Then without touching me, she ran her hands around my body, "Your energy levels are magnificent, but I will have to talk to your mom about getting some crystal jewelry to protect you from bad energy."

Mom could see that I'm feeling a bit uncomfortable with all this attention. She breaks in, "Maddi, Star is in your room; you should go and say hi."

My mind races! Star is in my room. Who said she could go in there? My room is full of my private stuff. I race down to save my privacy.

TOO LATE!!!!!

Star is lying on my bed reading my diary! She looks over the top of the book as I burst into my room. Before she even says, "Hi Maddi," I rip my diary from her hands. She tries to snatch it back, "Come on, Maddi. It was just getting interesting!"

Star is an imposing sight, tall for her age with her dyed jet-black hair long on one side and almost shaved on the other side. She has multiple earrings and a fake tattoo on her arm (at least I think it is fake), and a stud in both of her eyebrows.

I clutch my diary to my chest and screech, "How dare you read my diary; it's private!"

"Not anymore," she responds with a smirk. "Don't worry, Maddi. I'm not interested in your dull little school dramas. My life is much more interesting," snarled Star.

At that moment, Mom arrived, "Come on, girls, we are going for lunch." Good timing. Mom, Star, and I were about to have our own version of wrestle mania.

On the trip to lunch, Mom and Demi constantly chatted while Star and I sat in the back seat – in total silence!

In the restaurant, things continued much the same until, in a moment of unexpected meanness, Star tips her glass of juice into my lap. I squeal as the cold liquid hits my thighs.

Finally, Mom and Demi stop talking. They both grab some napkins and start to try and soak up the mess.

The waiter comes over too and helps clean up the juice. He even replaces Star's drink.

Star keeps saying that she is sorry. I know she doesn't mean it.

Mom says, "Don't worry, dear, accidents happen."

Star gives me her best fake smile and winks at me. I feel like tipping my juice over Star's head but show some restraint and decide to wait for a better chance for revenge.

The meals arrive. Star and I both have nachos with little side dishes of sour cream and chili sauce. The chili sauce is in a bottle that looks like a soda bottle. Star announces that she needs to go to the bathroom, and I see my chance.

As the waiter goes past, I ask if I can swap my chili sauce for extra hot chili sauce. I think he feels sorry for me and rushes off to change the sauce bottles. I quickly switch it with the bottle next to Star's plate.

Star returns and grabs the extra hot sauce bottle, and dumps the whole lot over her nachos. She must be hungry, as she quickly scoffs two large mouthfuls of food into her mouth. Suddenly her eyes widen, and she starts to cough. I guess that the extra hot chili sauce is beginning to take effect.

While she is distracted, I hand her the second bottle of chili sauce. She thinks it is her soft drink and takes a large gulp. Her eyes bulge like some type of wild cartoon character, and she explodes. A mouthful of sauce and nachos flies across the table.

A bit hits Mom, but most of it splashes onto Demi. Needless to say, after that, lunch is over.

The ride home is pretty quiet, except for me munching my nachos and Star's occasional coughing and whimpering that her mouth is on fire.

The waiter put my nachos in a takeaway container and, with a wink, said, "Careful with that sauce."

Demi and Star head off in their car as soon as we got home.

Mom gave me a stern look and asked if I had anything to do with what happened at lunch.

I just smiled and replied, "I think those nachos had a dash of karma."

Mom screwed up her face, trying to work out what I had meant. Then she shrugged her shoulders, kissed me, and went downstairs.

Monday

D is for disaster!

D is also for devastated!

Today after school, the worst thing ever happened. Mom called me into the kitchen; Dad was already sitting at the breakfast table. Dad's normal happy smiling face had disappeared, replaced by a very sad mask. A glance at Mom revealed that her expression closely matched Dad's.

A million things raced through my mind!

Had they discovered I changed a C in Math on my last report card into a B with skillful use of a fine black marker?

Could it be that zombies are real, and we are the last humans left?

Or, was I adopted, and today I was to be returned to my rightful parents…the King and Queen of some European country?

Wrong!!!!!

Much worse!!!!!!

Mom and Dad haven't been getting along very well for the last few months, and they have decided to separate for a while.

There were tears all around, but Mom and Dad assured me they both still love me, and we would still be a family, although Dad would be going away for a while.

I felt sad when Dad left that night, as did Mom. We cried on each other's shoulders.

Dad had promised to contact us each day, and Mom said she believed Dad would be back. She said it was the stress of his job causing him to be sad.

True to his word, Dad calls or emails us every day, and I just hope we'll all be back together one day.

I don't want to say…D is for divorce!

2 Weeks Later...

Tuesday

I haven't written in my diary for a while. I've been missing Dad and so has Mom, so I've spent more time keeping her company. For a while, Mrs. Absolutely Positive lost her shine and sparkle, but we have both settled down now. Dad still contacts us every day, and even though he isn't here, he is still part of my life.

The funniest thing happened at school today in Math. My History teacher's nickname is Mr. Oscar...because he is always super grumpy! He reminds me of Oscar The Grouch from Sesame Street. He even has those big googly eyes behind his glasses, just like the Oscar puppet.

Anyway, in his normal grouchy way, he made everyone shift their seats so we weren't sitting with our friends. I ended up sitting between Bethany Barker (MG – short for a mean girl) and a boy called Justin Smithers. I haven't had a lot to do with Justin but have heard some of the "less kind" boys call him "Dustbin" rather than Justin.

That unfortunate name goes back to last year in my English class. Our teacher was a very young and pretty lady who was always beautifully dressed with perfect make-up and hair. So obviously I called her Miss Barbie!

Miss Barbie was quite a good teacher but was somewhat obsessed with neatness and cleanliness. Sometimes she would stop in the middle of a lesson to straighten the pencils and books on a kid's desk. She even had a bottle of hand sanitizer on her desk that she used every time after she touched our workbooks.

After lunch and playtimes, she would spray an air freshener around the room. And she would always say the same thing, "We don't want to be smelling all those sweaty bodies and foot odors all afternoon, do we children?"

Sometimes on particularly hot days, she would tip some of her perfume onto a tissue and hold it up to her nose to protect her delicate senses from her foul-smelling students. Do you get the picture? Miss Barbie is one delicate princess!

In her classroom, the desks are always perfectly arranged in groups of six. One day as Miss Barbie moved around the room, I saw her nose begin to twitch, and then her perfect face transformed into a grimace.

With a puzzled look, she slowly moved around the room, stopping at each desk and sniffing gently. "Does someone need to go to the bathroom?" she asks in her delicate sweet voice. She thinks one of us has let off a smelly fart.

Naturally, nobody responded. Everyone put their heads down and focused on their work. Miss Barbie continued to sniff around the room.

"There is a really bad smell in here somewhere," she announced loudly, with her sweet voice turning shrill as her delicate senses are assaulted by the smell.

This time a few kids responded that they could smell something bad too. Miss Barbie starts a more intensive sniffing campaign, moving from one group to another.

Finally, she returned to the group next to mine. In that group are three girls and three boys, one of the boys is Justin Smithers. She calls each of the kids out to the front of the class, one at a time, for a whispered conversation. I manage to just hear the words, "Are you sure you don't need to use the bathroom," as she talks to each of the kids. Miss Barbie does another circuit of the room before returning to the same group.

This time she starts going around the group, instructing each student to open their desk. Miss Barbie has a quick look and a big sniff and then moves onto the next desk. She's found nothing so far, and there are only two kids left, Justin and another boy.

Following Miss Barbie's instructions, Justin opens his desk

wide, and Miss Barbie takes a big sniff. She recoils in horror and takes two steps back.

Her perfect face is pinched up into a scowl. She holds her nose as she uses a ruler to poke around in Justin's desk. With the tips of her fingers, she lifts a plastic-wrapped item from the desk, it oozes and drips, and a disgusting stench floods the room.

Miss Barbie runs from the room, still clutching the stinking mess in her hand and making retching noises as she leaves.

Five minutes later, Mr. Sausage Nose – the principal, walks in and announces he will be taking the class as Miss Barbie has gone home sick.

After class, the kids are giving Justin a bit of a hard time for causing the stink.

He explains that he hadn't finished his hot dog at lunchtime, so he had hidden it in his desk, intending to eat it in class while the teacher wasn't looking.

It could not have stunk that bad…just from lunchtime. We saw that it was starting to decompose, turning to mush!

Justin's mouth opened wide; he went white, "Oh no, it wasn't my hot dog from today. It was a hamburger from about three months ago! I forgot about it."

Justin couldn't smell it because he had his nose broken twice playing football, and the injury had destroyed his sense of smell. And that is, unfortunately, how Justin got to be called Dustbin by some of our nastier class members.

Anyway, here I sit between Justin and Mean Girl as Mr. Oscar fires lightning-fast questions around the room.

I follow the standard 'avoid being picked to answer

questions' tactics, appearing to listen intently and making no eye contact with the teacher, and nodding wisely when someone else answered correctly.

Then suddenly, Mean Girl jabs me in the ribs with her sharp and boney elbow. I give an involuntary "oomph" as I double over in pain and surprise.

That's when I make my mistake. I panic and look up to see if Mr. Oscar has heard me. Bad mistake! Our eyes lock! EYE CONTACT! Oh, no....

"Right Maddi, next question is yours," snaps Mr. Oscar.

Panic overtakes me; my pulse is beating faster than a speeding bullet. Here comes the question. I hold my breath, trying to focus.

"What is the bluzen dinky xyt24 62536477flmkjqu," he asks. At least, that is what it sounded like to me.

My "I don't know" response gets a swift reaction.

"I'll see you at lunchtime for some extra work, Maddi."

I steal a glance at Mean Girl, and she gives me a self-satisfied smirk while poking her tongue at me.

Justin asks for a loan of a blue coloring pencil, and I hand it over with a smile. As I work on my assignment, I notice that Justin is using my pencil for NON-coloring purposes.

First, he uses the non-sharpened end to give both his ears a good clean out; then, he does a bit of exploration of his right nostril. It's hard to be sure, but I think I see a little green thing on the end of my pencil.

Justin returns my pencil with a "thanks."

I reply, "Pop it on my desk." After a while, I 'accidentally' knock the pencil off my desk onto the floor.

I don't want to hurt Justin's feelings, but there is NO WAY that I am going to put my fingers on that germ-covered pencil ever again! The cleaners can have that one, they wear gloves when they pick up stuff from the classroom floor, so I know they won't catch anything.

Mean Girl must have seen me drop the pencil off my desk because she suddenly swoops down and picks it up. Why, at this precise moment in world history, does Mean Girl decide to be nice to me? I'm wracking my brain to think of reasons why I don't want the pencil back without revealing the truth. If she knew why I didn't want the pencil back, she might use that information to tease Justin.

No need to worry! Mean Girl waggles the pencil at me and sneers, "Was this yours? Well, not anymore. This is my favorite color."

As well as being a bully and a generally unlikeable person, Mean Girl has another off-putting habit. She chews on things – her fingers, her ruler, the ends of her hair, and today she has something else to chew on…the end of my pencil.

GROSS! She has a good chew, and I can't help but snigger. She hears me and turns and sticks even more of my pencil into her mouth to chew on. I laugh even more. A confused look shows on Mean Girl's face. Me laughing was not the reaction she expected.

I decide not to tell her why I am laughing, not today…maybe another time when she is being a bully. It's so funny that I even manage to get through my lunchtime detention with a smile on my face.

Thursday

Science is looking interesting today. Mr. Facebook is taking our lesson in the actual science lab! There are beakers and test tubes and Bunsen burners, and bottles of chemicals labeled with A, B, C, and D on each of the tables.

Naturally, Shelby and I grab a table together. Our table is at the far back corner of the room near a window. Unfortunately, it is a bit hard to hear Mr. Facebook from our table as he is demonstrating what to do from the front of the room.

Mr. Facebook is on fire (well, not really on fire) and teaching a great lesson. He has us mixing chemicals and stuff and creating all kinds of exciting reactions like clouds of colored steam and popping bubbles bursting out of beakers.

The whole class is really involved and having fun. To be honest, we are all being a bit too noisy because the activities are so exciting.

Mr. Facebook announces that our last activity can be a little dangerous and to listen and watch carefully. He starts giving instructions on how to measure out quantities of different chemicals.

In our far corner, Shelby and I are struggling to hear his instructions. When he measured chemical C...we couldn't tell if he said 15mls or 50mls. I went to the front to ask him.

Just as I got there, he pulled out his phone. He had heard a Facebook notification.

"Excuse me," I asked politely, "did you say 15 or 50?"

His attention is firmly fixed on his phone now, and he answers, "Yes" to my question. Even I know that "yes" isn't the correct answer. I repeat the question.

Mr. Facebook is now typing away on his phone and, if possible...giving me even less attention. "50!" he snarls, followed by, "get back to your table and do your experiment."

I go back to the table and tell Shelby he said 50. She looks doubtful, but what can we do? We start to combine our chemicals into one large beaker—first chemical A and then chemical B. We hesitate as nothing has happened. The group at the next table has just finished pouring in chemical C. From their beaker, we see a puff of smoke and hear a loud pop.

That doesn't look too scary, so I grab the 50ml of chemical C that we have already measured out and pour it into the beaker (containing the other chemicals). I'm holding the beaker in my left hand, watching it closely. I can see the mixture of chemicals bubbling up, heading towards the top of the beaker.

If the group next to us had a puff of smoke...we have our own little nuclear bomb mushroom cloud happening. The bubbly chemicals are about to spill over the side of the beaker! No way am I going to let that toxic brew touch my fingers! The only place I can see to dump it is the waste paper basket next to our table.

I toss the beaker like an extreme basketball shot. The beaker lands in the basket, and seconds later, there is an extremely loud bang, followed by even more smoke pouring from the bin.

The smoke is quickly drifting across the classroom. The loud bang has finally managed to draw the attention of Mr. Facebook from his phone. He gazes in stunned horror at the room rapidly filling with smoke.

Finally, he screams, "Get out, FIRE!" Everyone panics and runs for the door. Mr. Facebook hits the fire alarm on his way out of the building.

The Principal looks crazed, ordering everyone to evacuate all the school buildings. Soon our class is joined on the athletics field by the whole school. I sit listening to the sound of approaching fire trucks.

Once the all-clear signal was given, Mr. Facebook marched me up to Mr. Sausage Nose's office and firmly laid the blame on me.

I sit in the chair outside his office, waiting for my mom.

When Mom arrives, I try to explain what happened. But Mr.

Sausage Nose keeps interrupting me, saying how no other group had any problems. Mr. Facebook had told him that I wasn't listening, and that is the reason why I added way too much of the chemical.

When I tried to tell Mr. Sausage Nose how the teacher was on the phone instead of answering my question, he praised Mr. Facebook for having the sense to use his personal phone to ring the fire and rescue.

He said that if it hadn't been for his quick thinking and action…I could have burned down the whole school. "That's why he had his phone out Maddi, you must be confused," he said sternly.

"Mom, this is so unfair. It's not my fault. I'm telling you the truth!" I shouted.

The principal started to tell Mom that I would be suspended for 4 weeks for my actions.

To my shock, my mom butted in, raising her voice, "My daughter does NOT lie! She will not be suspended! We are moving to a new school." She grabbed me by the hand and stormed out of the office.

As we drove away, Mrs. Absolutely Positive simply said, "Maddi, don't worry, there are plenty of lovely schools to go to. There is a silver lining to every cloud of smoke."

And that's why I'm heading to my next adventure in 'My New School.'

BOOK 2

MY NEW SCHOOL

Monday

The beautiful blonde hippy woman screamed as the ninja assassin reached towards her. But just in time, her slightly more beautiful and very cool 12-year-old daughter triple backflipped in between the ninja and her Mom…blocking his killer strike.

Well, not really.

In fact, the blonde hippy woman is actually my mother. My Mom is highly alternative, with a Capital A…I hope we fit in here!

And the ninja assassin is really Mr. Jones, and he appears to be rather friendly for a school principal. He greeted me with a huge smile and a high five. In fact, I think that will be a much better name for my new principal, Mr. High Five.

I am the 12-year-old girl who backflipped to save my mother. Okay, I've got a very active imagination. To be honest, I'm not beautiful, but a bit of a plain Jane, and I'm kind of almost cool, but not quite. I do like to think of myself as a child genius and funnier than a Bugs Bunny cartoon.

This is my new school, Harper Valley Elementary. I liked my old school. It was a pretty good school…before the explosion and fire. Don't get me wrong. I'm sure it will be good again, once the repairs are finished.

How would I know that mixing a bit of this with a bit of that would cause an explosion? I bet the inventor of dynamite wasn't asked to leave his school!

Mom and Dad split a couple of months before my invention incident. After the incident, it was suggested that my Mom should find a school more suitable.

This wasn't a great start to the year!

My Mom, I call her Mrs. Absolutely Positive, says this is just another small step on the journey of life, and as one door closes…another will open.

Going to a new school, where I don't know anyone, where I don't know where anything is, or any of the teachers, is "a great opportunity" for me, according to my Mom.

Now you know why I call her Mrs. Absolutely Positive. She thinks that hanging a crystal around my neck will protect me and solve all my problems. The only way that crystal will help me is if I swallow it and have to be taken out of here in an ambulance.

Mr. High Five has been droning on for about 20 minutes now and has introduced his Deputy.

No high fives or even a smile from her. Just a not so brief summary of the 5000 and 1 rules of Harper Valley School, complete with the details of punishments. I think I'll call her Mrs. She Who Runs The School.

Oh goody, we have finally finished the enrolment, now I get to go to my new class and meet the teacher…and be stared at and evaluated by thirty other kids.

7A is my new class; the A is for amazing, says my new teacher. She prattled on for a good ten minutes about how much I will enjoy my new class, how lovely the children are, and how learning is fun. And we'll be doing so much learning that it will be fun every second of every day.

Yeah sure. Five hours cooped up in a small room with 30 other children, all with various body odor problems with activities ranging from mind-melting boredom to fun extension work. You know, the kind of work that makes you feel like you are going insane. I think I'll call her Miss Learning Is Fun.

After careful consideration on how to further destroy my life, Miss Learning Is Fun chooses a lovely seat for me next to what appears to be a living fossil, "The Cave Man". Burt is about 10 foot tall, 10 foot wide, and has more hair on his knuckles than I have on my head. He raises his eyebrows and grunts what I think is *hello*, as I take my seat.

Just like Mom said, "A fresh new start will be marvelous for you."

As I sit in the shadow of Burt, I scan the class for signs of intelligent life forms. I see the usual standard mix for any class. The popular girls, the footy boys (that explains some of the odors), the nerds, and scattered around the room are the weirdos.

A few kids seem almost normal and could be worthy of further investigation—especially a tall, dark and handsome boy...who actually appears to be able to read.

As I sit eating dinner that night, my organic tofu and enough salad to feed an army of bunnies, Mom gushes, "I bet you had a great day."

"How many new friends did you make?" I mumble "none," but she seems not to hear, but continues about how I should make it a goal to make a new friend every day, so by the end of the year...the whole school will be my friend.

Yeah, right, then perhaps I could move on to the billions in China. After our compulsory ritual of 30 minutes of yoga and meditation, Mom sends me off to bed with a "remember the early bird gets the worm" talk. I wonder what girls with normal mothers are doing—eating a cheeseburger while watching TV probably, oh those poor, poor children.

Tuesday

I HATE swimming!

Oh, I can swim okay. I can even put on my swim cap and adjust my goggles so they don't become mini swimming pools for my eyes. Some kids swim like dolphins, sleek and smooth through the water. However, I swim more like a hippo, just my eyes showing above the surface and a LOT of kicking and splashing! I can make the 50, but if you come to watch, you might just want a snack to tide you over as you wait for me to finish.

After my school swimming lesson today, I HATE SWIMMING even more!

It all started going wrong when Mum presented me with a new swimsuit. It was the height of fashion, about 100 years ago! You know the type, a lovely floral number with some frills in all the wrong places. I know that sounds horrible, but I hid my feelings from my Mom. She always tries her best. So, I smiled and thanked her. I even kept smiling when she gave me a matching swim cap.

Mrs. Absolutely Positive then assured me that they are a one-off outfit, totally unique, and will help me to stand out from the crowd. Thanks, Mom, that's just what every 12-year-old girl wants to do, stand out and be different.

I know that all this sounds really sarcastic, but with you *Dear Diary*, I can say what I think. I am an expert at the blank look. Nobody can read my thoughts. But I have to tell someone. I have to get it all out.

My Mom may be an alternative (hippy clothes, a piercing on her nose, and a tattoo on her ankle), but she is very efficient. She has carefully and clearly labeled all my clothes and belongings with my name. It seemed an excellent idea at the time, before today, that is.

Swimming was our second lesson of the day, and we hurried out to the bus after English.

The trip on the bus is loud, smelly, and hot. Do kids who are 12 really sing 'The Wheels On The Bus'? Yes, they do at Harper Valley, and Miss Learning Is Fun cheerfully led them through each verse. Really? Have they not heard of the radio or a CD?

We finally arrive and have to share the change room with a class of little kids.

This is when my first mistake of the day happens. Do you know how your Mom always says to wear good undies when you go out? Well, I didn't. My undies had a couple of holes, but worst of all they had Dora The Explorer on them. (Mum thought they looked adorable when she bought them, she thought the picture was a Hawaiin girl, not a little kid's character.)

Anyway, as I changed into my unique and attention-grabbing swimsuit, I became aware of the joy and amusement I was causing. Little girls and my classmates were all staring and laughing at my swimmers; some even pointed, in case I was in any doubt, that I was the focus of their attention.

I hurriedly stuffed all my clothes into my bag, or so I thought, and ran outside waiting at the edge of the pool — my class on one side and the little kids on the other side.

Then I saw the pool attendant walking out of the change rooms, a pair of undies extended into the air on the end of her fingertips. I recognized them immediately. Then the whole scene went into agonizing slow motion.

She goes across to the little kids and holds the undies up. Nobody claims them, so she heads over to our class. She does a great job of holding them up. Dora is easily identifiable, and the holes clearly visible.

Her fingers are covering up the name tag, so she can't see my name. Thank goodness! Nobody is going to know that the ultimate in embarrassing undies is mine. What a relief. The attendant walks away, and now I can breathe again and focus on surviving swimming.

'Screeeeech'! The pool's loudspeaker system squawks to life. "Attention please, attention please, I have a lost pair of girl's underwear, they have a lovely picture of Dora The Explorer on both the front and back…hang on; there is a name tag, Maddi Bull, Maddi Bull, please come to the counter to collect your underwear."

I try to disappear into the cracks in the concrete but to no avail. Miss Learning Is Fun calls from the front of the line, "That's why it is so important to name everything, quick Maddi, go and collect your undies straight away."

The walk of shame begins. Past my class (most were sniggering), past the little kids (even they were smirking), and past the wrinklies who were doing their slow-motion water aerobics.

One of the little kids called out, "Cool undies!" Another yelled, "I love Dora too!" Great, I'm a legend with 5-year-olds!

I return to my class and prepare to face my next ordeal, the swim. Many laps later, I cuddle the lane rope and try to get my breath back. The little kids are in the pool now. At least I can swim better than them (well, most of them).

The swim coach calls us out of the pool. Now he wants us to dive in and retrieve plastic rings. Fantastic, I'm good at diving! I breeze through this. Then he makes it into a contest. Two kids at a time, the winner moves on, and the loser is eliminated. Round after round, I win. This is my big chance to impress my classmates. I can gain respect, be cool and make up for the undies incident.

It is down to the leader of the cool girls' group and me. Her name is Mandy the Mermaid (not her real name). The coach tosses the ring in and blows his whistle. We hit the water together. I kick as hard as I can and reach down. I grab it and raise my hand in triumph. Except when I look at Mandy the Mermaid, she is holding the ring in her hand. The faces of the class and coach have a strange look of horror pasted on them.

One of the little kids has had an accident. It isn't the plastic ring I am holding. I'm holding a ring of poo! I scream and toss it away. The looks of horror turn into howls of laughter. I feel like diving to the bottom to escape, but what is lurking underwater is even worse than facing my class.

"No, Mom, I didn't have fun at swimming. Can we move to the desert?"

Friday

Cooking today, no worries, I can cook toast, 2-minute noodles, and virtually anything you can reheat in a microwave oven.

I like the cooking class already. My teacher's name is Mrs. Muffin; her real name is Mrs. Moffat. As she went through the kitchen rules, I was warping her body into a muffin and dusting her with icing sugar.

Actually, she is excellent. She made us all put on hairnets. You should have heard the groans and whining from the cool girls. Covering up their shiny, gorgeous hair makes them look normal. Yaayyy!

Remember I told you about a tall, dark, and handsome boy who caught my attention on my first day? Well, obviously his name is Mr. Tall Dark and Handsome. Well, Mrs. Muffin paired me up with – Mr. Tall Dark and Handsome himself!!!! And a funny, geeky-looking girl called Gretel.

Things are starting to turn around. This might be my chance to impress. I look at the recipe and ingredients. Oops, no mention of reheating in the microwave. We have to make chicken in apricot sauce and vegetables. A bit more complicated than I had hoped for, but never fear, Gretel appears to know what she is doing. I think she is some kind of master chef. Already she is dicing and slicing, leaving me plenty of time to talk to Mr. Tall Dark and Handsome.

Soon Gretel has everything ready to go into the oven. I think I might let Gretel work with me every cooking lesson; she's fantastic!

As she pops the food into the oven, Mrs. Muffin tells her that her brother is sick and she has to go home early. I have to stop interrogating (I mean talking to) Mr. Tall Dark and Handsome and take over.

It was then that I realized we were alone, and I had no idea what to do next — not the slightest idea of how long to cook the chicken dish for. I don't want to be uncool and let him know I am useless at cooking, so I just have to work it out. Let's see, noodles take 2 minutes max, and the microwave meals mum cooks take 10 minutes. The school ovens are big and fan-forced, so they'll probably cook heaps faster. So, I'm guessing 5 minutes should do it. But just to be safe, I'll leave it in for 6 minutes.

What a star! I pull the dish out in 6 minutes, and we are the first group to finish. Mrs. Muffin is impressed. None of the other groups are anywhere near finished. Is that the smell of an A for cooking???

She decides to do a taste test and scoops a big spoonful into her mouth. All the kids gather around in awe. As she chews, her face contorts, and she seems to gasp for air. Suddenly, she violently spits out my apricot chicken all over Mr. Tall Dark and Handsome, and several nearby students.

"That chicken is RAW!!!" she screams. So, cooking class ends early, looks like an E on my report for cooking. Mr. Tall Dark and Handsome stares at me in disbelief and walks away. And Mrs. Muffin now has a new name, Mrs. Chew and Spew.

Thank goodness I have the weekend to get over my cooking failure.

Monday

After a short interview with Mr. High Five and She Who Rules the School, I am cleared of deliberately trying to poison the cooking teacher and am merely found guilty of gross stupidity. The principal gives me a high five as I leave. And the deputy quietly snarls at me, "I'm keeping an eye on you."

I hurry off to my English class, but by the time I get there, it has already started. The teacher looks grumpy already. I like to call him Mr. Albert because his frizzy wild hair looks like it was done by Albert Einstein's hairdresser.

"Madonna, we've just finished reading everyone's essays on 'The Merchant of Venice,' pass me yours, and I'll read it because we need to get on with today's work."

I fumble in my bag for my English book but accidentally pull out my diary instead. It is covered in the same dark pink paper that Mom covered all my books in. Mr. Albert starts to read in his loud, clear voice. Oh no! I made this diary entry last night when I was multi-tasking my English homework and diary dreaming.

The quality of mercy is not strained…but falls like the gentle rain. Mercy, I wish that Mr. Albert would give me some mercy and sit me next to that hunky Richard Jones. I love his gorgeous hair and those hazel-brown eyes. Mr. Albert comes to a stop, and there is a moment of complete silence before the whole class bursts into spasms of laughter and cheering.

The only people not laughing are Richard Jones and me. We appear to be having a blushing competition with no clear winner.

Oh, the teacher isn't laughing either. He asks me who Mr. Albert is. I tell him it is just my imagination. The bell rings, and I try to disappear to the darkest corner of the library. I've decided to research if NASA needs any 12-year-old girls to send into space TODAY!!!

Lunch...the loneliest word for losers like me. The student body seems to be divided into two groups. Those who think I am a complete idiot and just laugh at me. And those who think I am a crazy fool and want to stay away from me. I sit in the far-eating corner, alone with my bean and tofu salad. It always seems that my life is destined to appear on the TV show - World's Worst Disasters.

As I sit with my head down, a shadow falls across me. I don't dare look up; it is probably someone who has come to tease me about one of my stupid antics.

"Hi, that looks like a nice salad." I look up and see Gretel smiling down at me. She sits beside me and tells me how she feels sorry for me because of the cooking incident and the diary mistake. She continues on about how we should work together in the next cooking class because she can help me. I look at her in shock. Is she insane!!!!

Lunchtime passes quickly as we talk about our families and the friends, we wish we had.

Hey Mom, I think I may have made a new friend.

Wednesday

New Day...New Lesson.

I sit confidently beside Gretel in Science. My history with science is not good, and that's why I'm letting Gretel take the lead role.

Our science teacher looks like a scientist with thick red hair. She also teaches me math (well, she can try!) I think I'll call her Mrs. Red.

Anyway, all is going well...Gretel and I have gathered the test tubes, beakers, bunsen burner, matches, safety goggles, and an assortment of materials. Quickly we use our superior skills to read through the procedure and set up our equipment.

Mrs. Red has positioned herself in front of our bench. She's keeping an eye on the pair of jocks that appear to be having trouble. What a pity she has her back to us and can't see what a great job we are doing.

Gretel skillfully mixes the substances in the beaker of tap water while I time how long it takes to dissolve. Next, we heat the bunsen burner to see how long it takes to dissolve in hot water.

I play it safe and leave the lighting of the bunsen burner to Gretel. Perhaps I shouldn't have told her about my experiences at my last school. Four matches later and still no flame. I urged Gretel to put the match closer. But she put it too close and jams the match into the gas nozzle, where it gets stuck!

That's when I have a brain wave. I'll turn the gas up full blast, and that will probably blow the match out of the nozzle. I probably should have told Gretel about my plan. Just as the gas handle reaches maximum flow, Gretel lights another match. The stuck match shoots out and hits the flame on Gretel's match with a huge whoosh!!!!!

So, there you have it. Our bunsen burner is now a flame-thrower that any Xbox gamer would be proud of. We watch in horror as the flame races towards Mrs. Red's head. The flame just reaches the ends of her wild hair. I turn the gas off, and Gretel throws the beaker of water at her hair.

Mrs. Red turns around and yells, "What are you girls doing!!!!"

Gretel apologizes, "Sorry, Miss, I tripped and spilled the water." She didn't know what had just happened. She didn't know that her hair had been on fire. "Well, hurry up, girls, you haven't even got your bunsen burner turned on yet," she snaps.

I mouth a "thank you" to Gretel, and she smiles and says, "That's what friends are for."

The rest of the day passed without incident. After the close shave in science, I kind of like boring.

Monday

PE lesson time with Mr. Arnie. Now Mr. Arnie is BIG, and I mean BIG in a fit, muscular way. I feel that Mr. Arnie is a much better name than Mr. Jones (his real name) as he does look like the school's own Terminator.

He walks us over to the climbing wall. I think he plans to terminate me! Great an activity that combines my fear of heights and my natural lack of coordination. What can possibly go wrong? I hope the school nurse isn't busy.

Mr. Arnie puts us into teams, and guess what!!! Mr. Tall Dark and Handsome is my partner! I tell him that my climbing experience is limited to climbing out of bed in the morning. So, he volunteers to go first. What a gentleman! He is quite lovely.

Today is my chance to make an impression and connect with him. Mr. Tall Dark and Handsome puts on his safety harness and gets ready to climb. And I am his safety person; I have to hang onto the safety rope to make sure he doesn't slip off the handholds and fall to the ground.

Well, Mr. Tall Dark and Handsome isn't exactly Spiderman, but he moves pretty well and rapidly approaches the top. Soon he'll be back on his way down, and my fringe is hanging in my eyes. I try to move my hair; it needs a flick back. The trouble is that both my hands are on the safety rope. He's climbing well and looking very secure. I'll just hold the rope with one hand and fix my hair.

The cry from above and jerk on the rope happens at the same time. The rope whirls through my hand before I can get both hands back on. Mr. Tall Dark and Handsome only falls about a body length, but he manages to bounce his head against the wall quite hard.
Mr. Arnie rushes over and helps lower him to the ground. Mr. Tall Dark and Handsome (Mr. TDH) is quite good about it. He says the swelling black eye doesn't hurt that much. He tells me that it could happen to anyone.

Then he helps me put on my harness and gives me advice on which handholds to use first. He is sooooo nice!!!! I want to impress him and set out determined to reach the top. I'm going well. This isn't going to be as hard as I thought.

I risk a quick look down at him. BIG MISTAKE!!! I seem so high, my heart begins to pound, and my hands start to sweat. I can't move my legs. I'm frozen to the spot.

I'm like one of those little lizards that grip to a wall, motionless, so predators can't see them. Except my strength is running out. My arms and legs begin to shake. Mr. TDH yells encouragement so does Mr. Arnie.

I glance down again and realize I'm the last one on the wall, and the rest of the class has finished and are gazing up at me.

I must go on; I use all my willpower and reach up with my right hand to the hold. My fingers brush it but slip off. I stretch further and push with my legs using all my remaining strength. My sweat-soaked fingers on my right hand slip off the handhold. Time seems to stand still for a few seconds; I can hear my heart thumping.

Then I try to reach the hold again, but my frantic efforts cause my upper body to swing out from the wall. In a flash, I'm hanging upside down! Thank goodness Mr. TDH is better on the safety ropes than me.

I look down to see where I am, but I can't see anything. My loose gym shirt has fallen over my face.

The crowd below can't see my blushing face, but they can see my sports bra! And I stayed upside down for 2 minutes while they lowered me down to the ground.

The gasps of shock as I first fell have quickly turned to laughter. If laughter is truly the best medicine, then my classmates are going to be very healthy.

I wanted to make an impression on Mr. TDH, but not this way!

When I finally reach the ground, Mr. TDH turns away while I readjust my top and then assures me that I'm okay with a concerned look in his eyes.

Maybe today wasn't a COMPLETE disaster after all.

Friday

"Wake up darling, I've got a surprise for you!" calls my mom (with her way too happy for 7 o'clock *in the morning* voice). A surprise!

The last surprise Mom got for me was a week-long Buddhist enlightenment course, where they shaved my head, fed me grains, nuts and vegetables, and had me either chanting or sitting in silence all day long. I had to wear a hat for six months until my hair grew back!

Reluctantly, I head downstairs to find Mom smiling and holding up a costume. "Try it on," she says. Now I don't know about you, but I never win an argument with my mom, so I figured I can spend 15 minutes asking why saying I'm too old to dress up in costumes and that I don't want to try it on or I can just do it now. I put it on. The red, white, and blue Supergirl costume is pretty amazing. I love the shiny red boots and blue cape. Actually, the shorts and top look pretty good on me. And the eye mask really sets off the costume.

As I stand there looking like an aspiring student from Super Hero College, Mom pulls out the camera and starts clicking away.

I check myself in the mirror. Super Hero red and blue just might be my colors. And, in a strange way, the eye mask does seem to accentuate my eyes. As I stand there admiring myself, I suddenly think...why has Mom got me this costume?

When I ask her, she explains that she saw in the school's newsletter that today is the dress-up day. I didn't know that. I ask Mom if she is sure, and she is absolutely certain! I go looking for the newsletter, but in her efficient and environmentally friendly way, she has put it in the recycling bin, which was collected yesterday.

Oh well, I do look good, and I'm sure Mr. TDH will think so too.

Mom even offers to drop me off at the school gate so I don't crush my cape on the school bus. I'll get there early, giving more people the chance to see how fantastic I look.

I strut into the school grounds with my cape billowing in the breeze. The first few kids I see don't have costumes on; they stare at me. Some people never join in on days like this. I wait near my classroom and watch as more and more kids arrive.

Problem! So far, nobody else has a costume on! By the time the bell goes, I'm hiding in the toilets. And I still haven't seen any other costumes.

I wait for a few more minutes to let the hall clear and then rush into my classroom. As I burst through the door, someone has left their bag lying just inside the doorway. I trip over it and fly through the air in my best Supergirl pose.

The class burst into laughter (they are getting healthy again) while mercifully, my cape falls over my face. The laughter dies down.

Miss Learning Is Fun starts clapping and smiles at me. "Wow, Madonna, what a creative entry into the room, but the dress-up day isn't until next week, dear."

At home that afternoon, Mom says, "I bet you had a great day, did everyone like your costume?" "Yes, Mom, I did stand out...thanks to you." She smiled at me with such a look of love, "No need to thank me, dear. That's what moms are for."

***

Friday

Two weeks have passed, and I've had NO dramas!

And no, I didn't dress up the following week.

It is so nice to be normal.

Mr. TDH has talked to me a few times; he's super friendly!

Monday

On my way to lunch today, I saw two lines at the student center. I wonder what I didn't hear about this time. I notice Gretel, three from the front of one of the lines. Ignoring the dirty looks, I slink down next to her and ask why she is lining up. She tells me you have to put your name down if you want to have a School Fair, and you're happy to help out on the day. She tells me how great it will be, "We'll have carnival rides and junk food galore. You've got to put your name down!" "Just line up with me."

The girl behind Gretel hisses at me and gives me a dirty look. So I go to the back of the line, behind about 30 kids.

After a few minutes, Gretel gives me a wave as she walks off. This is going to take FOREVER!!!! I look at the other line, it is much shorter, so I swap over. Honestly, some people have no brains! The line I left is still so long, and the one I swapped to is almost empty. I quickly put my name down and go and sit with Gretel to have lunch.

After lunch, when I'm happily daydreaming in English, Mr. Vale, the art teacher, enters our classroom. Mr. Vale is tall and slightly stooped. His head is balding. He has a big fat nose that is out of proportion with the rest of his face. The way he moves with his head thrust slightly forward and his black beady eyes kind of reminds me of a bald eagle. So naturally, I call him Mr. Eagle. Now

Mr. Eagle is VERY intense and, to be honest, a little scary. Most art teachers are all light and happy, dancing and singing their way around the school. But not Mr. Eagle!

He moans and groans a LOT and only seems happy when he is failing some poor kid for their lack of artistic skills.

Mr. Eagle holds a list of names and announces the following people are to report to the hall before school tomorrow for auditions in the school musical, Swan Lake. You can imagine my horror when he called out my name. A mistake! A horrible mistake!! I can't sing!!! And I can't dance!!!! Me in a musical, no way!

I raise my hand. The beady eyes swivel to me, and I nervously tell Mr. Eagle that there has been a mistake. I didn't sign up for the musical.

He struts over to me. His hot and coffee-smelling breath in my face, "Is this your handwriting?" he snarls. I've stopped breathing; it is my signature. My head drops, and I nod my head yes.

Mr. Eagle then launches into a speech about commitment and following through with promises. Then it hits me, two lines! I didn't put my name down for the school fair; I put it down for the musical.

I told Mom when I got home. I hoped she might ring him.

But no, she thinks I'll be brilliant in a musical. She went on and on about how she wished she would have had this fantastic opportunity when she went to school.

Tuesday

I got to the hall on time. All the talented kids were waiting outside. I felt so out of place! Mr. Eagle sits on a chair in front of the stage and calls us in one at a time. We had to go on stage and sing a song from a songbook on a stand. I'm about mid-group, and I feel like throwing up.

The girls before me are warming their voices up. They sound like they should be competing on American Idol.

Finally, my turn arrives. I trip on the stairs on the way up to the stage and knock the stand over. A glance at Mr. Eagle shows those beady black eyes staring at me. No smile, no encouragement.

My voice changes pitch as I struggle through the first few lines of the song. "Enough," he shouts. I ask if I can go now, and he gives me a second helping of his commitment speech and tells me to wait to the left so that I can try out for a dancing part.

As I wait for the singing auditions to end, I check out the dancing girls. They all have two things in common, dancing shoes and leotards. I get the feeling that I am the only person here who's dancing experience only consists of dancing in front of the TV to the Wiggles.

Eventually, Mr. Eagle calls us onto the stage. He wants us all to dance together at the same time. Phew!!!! What a relief! I can hide at the back. He quickly shows us a "simple" routine that we have to perform.

The music starts, and everyone takes four quick steps to the left, except me. Unfortunately, I go to the right. Then we had to move forward four steps and twirl. I collide with the two girls in front of me and send them sprawling to the floor.

"Enough!" roars Mr. Eagle.

"Will I go now?" I meekly ask him.

I get the commitment speech again, and he tells me to wait off stage.

P.s. Two months later, after many rehearsals, we finally put on Swan Lake. Mum picks me up at the back of the hall after I've removed my make-up and changed out of my costume.

"Oh, Madonna, I was so proud of you. You were such a great tree," Mom gushes.

Wednesday

I stand gazing at the noticeboard.

Keep Our School Clean POSTER Competition, reads the notice. A one-day free pass for three people for Waterslide World is the prize for the winning entry.

As I stand there dreaming, Gretel rocks up. "We should have a go at making a poster," she prompts me. Then Mr. TDH arrives with his smile and asks if he can work with us on making a poster.

Going to Waterslide World with my two friends, now that would be very cool!

Later, as we sit around and brainstorm ideas, we discover Mr. TDH is a computer whiz. He is highly skilled in computer graphics and editing pictures. Just what you need to create a winning entry.

With a shy smile, Mr. TDH suggests we need a superhero to clean up rubbish on our poster and asks if he can get a few photos of me in my costume because I look so good in it.

WOW!!!!! Of course, I agree!

Thursday

After school, I change into my costume, and we get some shots.

Meanwhile, I come up with this little rhyme to go with the poster (inspired by Mom's favorite singer – John Lennon).

IMAGINE THERE IS NO RUBBISH...

ANYWHERE IN THE WORLD...

NO CHOKING TURTLES...

NO PAPER ON THE GROUND...

IMAGINE ALL THE PEOPLE...

PICKING UP ALL THEIR JUNK...

WHAT A CLEAN PLACE IT WOULD BE...

SO CLEAN FOR YOU AND ME.

BTW, Mom loves this! I think it is a bit corny, but I can't think of anything else.

In no time at all, with Mr. TDH's skills, we have a great poster entered into the competition. And we are getting closer!

Monday

At last, we reach the day they announce the winners of the poster competition. All the students are gathered in the hall, waiting expectantly.

Mr. High Five, high fives his way to the center stage with a sheet of paper in his hand. I close my eyes and hope. Mr. High Five announces we have many great entries, but only one can win. "And the winner is...."

I open my eyes to see our poster on the data projector screen. Gretel's screaming drowns the rest of his words. But it doesn't matter, we have WON!!!!

Gretel, Mr. TDH, and I go up to the stage where Mr. High Five shakes our hands and presents us with the free pass.

I can't believe it! I'm on stage, and everyone in the hall is clapping and cheering for me. And I'm standing next to my two best friends.

You know, I think I'm going to love my time at Harper Valley School.

Sunday

The day finally arrives. Yes, Gretel, Mr. Tall Dark, and Handsome, and I take on Waterslide World. I am both excited and nervous. The three of us have free passes for Waterslide World.

According to the website, the biggest and best waterslides in the world feature *the longest black hole, fully enclosed waterslide ever built.*

I was so excited about winning - but now the day is here, I am worried. You see, I have always had a bit of fear about heights and enclosed spaces. The biggest waterslides equal **high waterslides with big drops**. And fully enclosed black hole slide equals **dark enclosed space** equals **FEAR FACTOR OF 10!!!!!**

Mom drops us off at Waterslide World just as it opens.

The attendant collects our passes and issues us with waterproof armbands complete with a barcode that gives us access to a locker to put our money and dry clothes in. We quickly put our valuables and dry clothes in the locker and just keep our towels with us.

Mom lathered us up with sunscreen before we came, and we all are wearing Lycra wet shirts, so we don't have to worry about getting sunburnt.

Most of the slides end in the same pool. It is enormous and has a marked-off area where you can swim if you want and a shallow section for little kids. Around the edge of the pool are a heap of deck chairs. We figure we might want to have a rest later, so we leave our towels spread out on three of the deck chairs.

Then we check out the park map and head for our first slide. It is a slide called The Terror Tower. It is an open slide and, despite its name, doesn't seem that high. We walk up the steps, and this takes a lot longer than I expected.

Finally, we reach the top, and Mr. TDH starts raving about the view. He keeps pointing out the landmarks we can see… I nod and smile but stop looking after the first one. This ride is a lot taller than I thought.

We wait for our turn. Mr. TDH is rapidly turning into Mr. Talkative, while Gretel is strangely quiet. As I look at Gretel, I notice that she is also very pale. When I asked her if she is okay, she gushes out how she has never been to an amusement park and is feeling scared. As I try to calm her and tell her how I'm scared, Mr. TDH listens intently.

"Thank goodness," he finally says, "I thought I was the only one who was scared."

Suddenly it's our turn, and the attendant hands us a foam mat to sit on to go down the slide. Mr. TDH bravely volunteers to go down first and rapidly disappears from sight. Gretel goes next. And I can tell when she reaches the bottom because that's when her screaming stops. Then it's my turn. I go swooshing down the slide…as fast as a rocket. My ride is over before I know it, and I splash into the pool at the end.

"That was great!" I yell to Gretel and Mr. TDH, who are waiting for me in the pool. (Mr. TDH has the loveliest smile.)

Perhaps I'm not such a chicken after all. Mr. TDH and Gretel seem to have overcome their fears, and together we run up the stairs to the second of many more slides on the Terror Tower. We try three other similar open slides and conquer all of them. Even though Gretel is having a ball, she still screams for the whole length of every slide. I didn't realize that the girl had such a great set of lungs.

Next, we head for an even bigger slide, which runs straight down with a couple of bumps along the way. It's called the River Of Doom. Really, where do they get these names from? Don't they know some little children could be scared! On this slide, you sit on a little rubber boat, one person on each side facing backward, and one lucky person gets to sit at the very back to face forwards. On the walk up to the top, I notice that the back seat is the way to go. Without fail, those people facing backward going down the slide - scream all the way down to the bottom.

I try to distract Gretel and Mr. TDH from watching the boats going down the slide. I pointed out the great view of the other slides, how well-made the steps are, and how close the sun is. However, I don't think my distractions have worked because when the attendant calls us forward for our go, both Gretel and Mr. TDH take off like rockets trying to get to the backseat first.

The floor of the boat is wet and slippery, and as Gretel and Mr. TDH each try to maneuver into the seat, I do the only sensible thing possible...I give them a huge shove sending them both sprawling into the boat while I slide into the back seat. They pick themselves up and glare at me as they sit in the backward-facing seats.

"You know, guys, this ride doesn't look half as scary when you can see where you are going," I chirp happily. Perhaps I shouldn't rub it in, but I did outsmart both of them, and I can't help myself.

The attendant gives me a peculiar smile as he starts to push the boat towards the edge. I guess he was impressed by how I outmaneuvered my friends to get the best seat.

Just as our boat is about to go over the edge, he looks at me and says, "Enjoy your ride." Then he spins the boat around so that Gretel and Mr. TDH are facing forwards, and now I am facing backward.

"ARRRHHHHH!!!!!" I scream all the way down. I sound as bad as Gretel. After that, I have to buy both Gretel and Mr. TDH an ice cream before they forgive me.

We decide to have a break; walking up all those stairs to the slides is pretty exhausting. We head to our towels and deck chairs. Gretel and Mr. TDH grab their towels and start to dry off.

But I have a problem. I feel like Goldilocks - someone has been sleeping on my deck chair. Someone is lying on my towel! And still is! A very large man, looking a bit like that famous wrestler - Hulk Hogan...and he is sound asleep on my deck chair.

Now I don't care about the deck chair, but I do care about my towel. It is a lovely blue and yellow one that Mom gave to me for my birthday last year.

Mr. Giant is asleep so deeply that he is snoring loudly, as loud as a jumbo jet taking off. About every fourth snore, he lets off a shuddering snort. Gross!!!!! A waterslide park is not a quiet place, so I don't know how he can sleep through all the noise, but his sleeping is about to stop.

I go to tap him on the shoulder when Mr. TDH grabs my arm and whispers, "Don't." Why is he whispering? I don't know. It would appear no noise could wake the sleeping giant? Mr. TDH tells me that he once read that waking a person in a deep sleep can be dangerous, as they could get a fright and lash out. Well, I don't want Mr. Giant lashing out. He could flatten all three of us accidentally.

Then I have a light bulb moment; I come up with a brilliant idea. A corner of my towel is hanging out over the edge of the deck chair; maybe I can pull it out from underneath him. I give it a tug; nothing happens. I tug as hard as I can, but still no towel.

I call Gretel and Mr. TDH over, and we all pull together with a mighty heave. The towel doesn't barge, nor does the giant, but we end up falling into a heap on top of each other.

Then Mr. TDH comes up with an even better idea and dashes off to buy a can of soft drink. Did I mention that it is a scorching day, and if you fell asleep lying in the sun - you would be feeling really, really hot! Anyway, we take turns in shaking up the can. Then we climb into the pool (luckily, the giant is on a deck chair close to the edge of the pool). Mr. TDH takes careful aim with the can and pops the lid. The last thing we see before we duck beneath the water is almost the entire contents of the can (as a frothy icy shower) spurting towards Mr. Giant's back.

We hold our breath for as long as we can, and when we pop up, Mr. Giant is standing up and wiping the soft drink off with my towel. He chucks the towel on the deck chair and storms off towards the park office with a fierce scowl on his face. We leap from the pool, grab our towels, and head for the opposite end of the park.

MISSION ACCOMPLISHED!!!! (In your head, play the Mission Impossible soundtrack.)

What a day, we have had so much fun - but before we go home, we have decided to tackle our fears and ride the black hole waterslide. Two minutes and 42 seconds of falling in total darkness! Yes, we are nuts!!!!!

We make the ascent to the top of the black hole with shaking legs and nervous bellies. We stand and watch the other people taking off for a while, trying to build up our courage. I noticed some kids using two mats, and I ask one teenage girl why. She tells me that it makes you go faster.

While I ponder this new information, Gretel starts grabbing at my arm and pointing at the steps. It's Mr. Eagle, the music teacher. I'd recognize that glistening bald head and weird walk anywhere. Mr. Eagle isn't our favorite teacher, and everyone finds those beady eyes that stare through you so intimidating.

Suddenly the pressure is on. We all want to go down the slide before Mr. Eagle arrives. Finally, we reach the front of the line, and Mr. TDH grabs a mat from the pile and launches himself down the tube. Gretel is next. With her face set in a grimace, she half falls and half jumps into the tube. As per usual, I can hear Gretel screaming all the way down. (Now that doesn't help with my confidence!)

I'm just not ready to go yet. The thought of being in the black tube is just overwhelming! I step aside and let two other people go. The attendant is a young teenage boy, and he is spending more time on his phone than supervising the slide. "Excuse me," I say, "can I grab an extra mat?" He mumbles sure without even looking at me. I look around and see that Mr. Eagle is going to end up standing in line behind me. That's it! I'm out of here! I want to go now and fast.

That's when I get a brilliant idea. I was going to grab two mats because that other kid said it makes you go faster. If I grab more than two mats, I should go even faster. The attendant isn't looking, so I start grabbing the mats and stacking them on top of each other. I start with one for my body and one for my legs, then add two more layers on top. Six mats - I'm going to fly down that tube. I sneak a quick glance back at Mr. Eagle. I don't think he has recognized me with my face plastered in sunscreen and my hair looking like a wet mop.

I get on the mats and try to push off, but nothing happens. I hear Mr. Eagles' voice behind me, "Hey kid, you've got too many mats!" Suddenly my mats start to move in the water flow going into the black hole, and I'm off! As I hit the first bend in the darkness – I scream! This is so fast and scary. I hit a sharp bend, and I feel the mats shift under me.

The next thing I know, I am tumbling along upside down, leaving a trail of mats behind me. Eventually, I stop, and in the dark, I grope around, and my fingers touch a mat. I pull it closer and sit on it. Hang on - why aren't I moving? It's the water flow, and it has slowed down to a tiny trickle - hardly enough to provide enough lubrication for the mat to slide.

I give a few pushes with my hands, and slowly I start to move again. Eventually, I reach the end. I stopped at the edge and have to jump out. Gretel and Mr. TDH are waiting in the pool and stare at me in bewilderment.

Then we hear the pool attendant on his walkie-talkie, "Tell the black hole attendant to stop the ride and don't let anyone else go down the slide as there must be a blockage."

Mr. TDH asks, "How could the slides get blocked?"

Before the attendant can answer, we all hear a faint boom, boom sound, and muffled yelling. We all look around, wondering where it is coming from.

Suddenly the attendant gasps, "Someone is trapped in the slide!"

He races off, and within minutes workers are tapping along the outside of the slide, trying to find where the trapped person is.

A worker has found the blockage mid-slide. They undo the massive bolts that hold the slide together. And this takes a long time.

As most of the park visitors stand around watching, they lift the top half of the section off. Revealing a stack of five mats blocking the slide and squashed up against the mats is a very angry-looking Mr. Eagle.

"It was that silly girl in front of me," he spits. "I told her she had too many mats."

I grab Mr. TDH and Gretel by their arms and quickly lead them over to grab our gear and head for the exit.

We have had a great day, but it is definitely time to leave!

He's Back!

I sense the presence in my room before I hear anything. I hold my breath and try to still my racing heart as I strain my ears to listen to any sound. I hear the floorboards creak. That's probably what woke me in the first place. I hear loud breathing, almost panting, and a scratching sound on the polished wooden floorboards of my bedroom. Slowly I gather my nerve and start to turn around in my bed to face it. My bed creaks, and I cringe and stop. The breathing seems to be closer now, so I quickly turn all the way over.

Before me stands a tall, black fur-covered creature with a mouthful of glistening white fangs. It's Tyson, my Dad's Great Dane dog. That can only mean one thing, Dad's back.

As I try to get out of bed, Tyson greets me with a low "woof" and happily wags his giant tail. In two quick wags, his tail sweeps all of my stuff from my dressing table. Tyson then leans against me as Great Danes tend to do and knocks me back into bed. He comes over and gives me a big sloppy lick before he trots out of my bedroom. I follow Tyson out to the lounge room to find Mom and Dad deep in conversation.

Mom and Dad split up about six months ago. I still speak to Dad every week on the phone. Mom, in her hippy alternative way, said Dad needed to rediscover himself, and it was just part of his life journey. I think he was just having a mid-life crisis (as did Mom), but I was still shocked to see him at our new home.

My Dad is a big tall man with brown hair. It is short now, it used to be very long, and he had a ponytail. I think he looks better with short hair, more "normal."

He also has a big booming voice. Seriously he could stun a cat at fifty yards and rattle windows at a hundred yards. That's why I often refer to him as Mr. Boom Boom. Think sonic boom but with a human sound.

Mom then announced the great news; Dad is coming back to live with us. I feel so happy; I love my Dad so much, and having my parents back together is so fantastic!

Sunday

Aloha! Hawaii Here We Come!

Dad has a great idea; we are going on a holiday to Hawaii. A chance to reconnect and harvest our energies so our family can achieve harmony again, so now you can see why Dad is married to my hippy alternative Mom or, as I call her, Mrs. Absolutely-Positive. Actually, he really shouldn't have had the ponytail cut off; my parents are like hippies. But that is cool for me (most of the time) because they are so loving and open.

I've never been on a plane, and to be honest, I feel a bit scared. I don't understand how something that big and heavy can fly in the air. When I asked, couldn't we just drive to Hawaii, Mom and Dad just laughed. After Dad explained that I would have my own DVD player to watch during the flight and that the cabin crew would bring me food and drinks, I decided it couldn't be that bad.

The takeoff was loud and fast, and the plane shook and shuddered as we left the ground. I held Dad's hand tight and was just beginning to relax when there was a loud thump as the landing wheels were retracted into the plane. Now apparently, everyone on board except me knew the thumping noise was normal. I, however, thought the tail of the aircraft had hit the ground as we went up off the ground, and I let out a loud scream.

I'm sure the whole plane burst out laughing. Sometimes I'm such a goose. Dad's laughter boomed out, and he had tears running down his eyes. Glad I could provide him some "free" entertainment!

Despite the DVD player, the flight is long and boring, and I eventually drift off to sleep.

I awake to a bad smell. As much as I love Dad, he eats too many baked beans and, as a result, often has a smelly gas problem. I try to ignore it and think of pleasant smells like maple syrup on pancakes, but it's no good. I have to say something. My "Dad! That's disgusting" comment comes out a bit too loud.

The lady in front turns around and apologizes because her baby has pooped her nappy, and she's just changing it. I don't know whose face went redder, mine or Dad's.

Finally, we arrive, and it's soooooo HOT! Our apartment is lovely on the tenth floor with a stunning view of the ocean. The ocean is beautiful with bluish-green water, dazzling white sand, and the white water of the broken waves.

So lovely to look at, but Dad informs me he has booked me into a learn-to-surf lesson first thing tomorrow morning. I don't want to go into the ocean on a surfboard!

Dad is big on trying new things and having new experiences. He thinks it helps you develop into a more confident person.

Really? Being battered by giant waves and chased by sharks is going to make me more confident.

Monday

Mom has hired a fluoro green helmet and a bright orange life jacket for my surf lesson. I think she is as horrified by the thought of me on a surfboard, out in the deep ocean, as much as I am.

I shuffle over to the lift, looking like an entrant in an extreme games' competition. In the lift, Dad lifts the helmet off my head and unties the life jacket, and stuffs them into his backpack. With a smile and a Hawaiian hang loose gesture, he says, "Let's just relax and enjoy the experience, but don't tell Mom."

Sometimes I think Dad is much cooler than Mom. Aaahh...well, that is until I looked at his boardshorts. My eyes must have popped because Dad smiled and asked, "So, do you like my new surfie, hang ten, cool dude boardies?" I smiled back and told him that he looked like the coolest father in the world.

I'm great at the surf lesson. I paddle well, jump up on the board with ease; I can even walk down to the nose and hang ten with my toes. Then the instructor spoils it all by making us leave the sand and go into the water. The water is so warm, which is good because I'm spending a lot of my time falling into it. Being in the water on the board is very different. The board seems to have come alive, and it moves to every bump and ripple in the ocean. When a wave comes, it becomes an evil assassin. The board rips out of my hands and hits me in the head. Maybe that helmet wasn't such a bad idea after all.

However, persistence pays off, and eventually, I manage to stand up and ride a wave for a little while. The instructor gives me a friendly wave and hoot, and I rush back out for another one. This is actually fun.

Thursday

After several lessons, I'm getting much better and venturing much further out. I love sitting on my board in the ocean, watching the surfers.

Today there are some excellent surfers doing tandem surfing. The guy takes off on the wave and then lifts his partner over his head, where she does all these gymnast-type poses. They often all catch the same wave and glide along together. It looks fantastic! I'd love to be able to do that, maybe next holiday.

The next wave that rolls in has me paddling for it, and five of these tandem surfers are paddling as well. I get up fast and start to glide along with the wave; it's the biggest I've ever caught. I'm so excited because I know Mom and Dad are videoing this.

I can hear Dad's booming voice shouting, "Go Madonna."

To my right, I can see the tandems surfing alongside me. The pair next to me is incredible; he just swung his partner through his legs to the back of the board.

I should have been looking where I was going because suddenly, I see another board floating by itself just in front of me (probably some uncool learner who can't stand up).

My board hits the loose board in the water, and I fly airborne straight onto the tandem board next to me. Amazingly I land on my feet but accidentally push the tandem girl off her board. She disappears with a splash.

But wait, it gets worse! The guy at the front (who is built like a giant) reaches back and grabs my hand. He pulls me closer and hoists me up into the air.

This can't be happening! It is like I've turned into a bird flying in the air with absolutely no control. I waver back and forth and yell at him to "PUT ME DOWN!!!!"

Finally, gravity wins, and I topple to the right, pulling my new partner with me. We take out the next surfing couple, who continue to take out the next pair in a domino effect until all five tandem surfing couples are down in the water.

Ten down. (Now, if that were bowling, I'd have a great score.)

I finally struggle into shore. I feel as though the water must be evaporating around me from the redness of my embarrassed face. Mom goes, "That was great, Madonna, and I got a great photo."

Monday

I Hate Bullies!

Back at school again, and everything's great. I'm looking tanned from my Hawaiian holiday and super fit. I have my Nike backpack, which all the kids are envious of, with its orange and purple panels and the lime green inserts on the straps. I love it!

I'm happily sitting in class next to my best friends, Gretel and Mr. Tall Dark and Handsome, when suddenly the deputy principal, Mrs. She Who Rules The School, bursts in the door. "Who owns this bag," she snaps in her usual breaking glass voice. As I said, everyone loves that bag of mine. She must have seen it on the racks outside the classroom and been so impressed she just had to know which lucky student owned it. Funny how she is only holding it with one finger and at arm's length, almost as though she finds my bag distasteful in some way.

When I raise my hand to claim ownership of the bag, she instructs me to come with her. As I follow her out the door, I wonder what those tiny white things are that seem to be falling off my bag.

When we get outside, she snarls at me, "Don't you ever clean your bag!"

I start to reply, "Of course I do, look how clean…."

When she lifts the flap, she tips my bag upside down and starts to shake it. More of those tiny white things begin to tumble out, and they look like they are wriggling. Then something bigger falls out. It looks like someone has painted my sandwich bag green.

Oh no, I finally recognize the object. It's a meat sandwich I didn't finish eating at lunchtime. Not today's lunchtime, but lunchtime a week ago - before my holiday. The green stuff is mold, and those little white things are wriggling because they're maggots, flies have laid eggs in my rotten food, and now maggots have hatched out.

After the last day of school, I threw my school bag in the corner without emptying it.

Mrs. She Who Rules The School leaves me to clean up my disgusting mess (as she calls it) while she rings my parents.

I'm not sure what's worse, getting all those wriggling maggots out of my bag or the laughter (and gasps of horror) as my class goes past on the way to the next lesson.

Finally, Mom, Dad, and I leave the school office after twenty minutes of lecturing from Mrs. She Who Rules The School about school standards and cleanliness. Mom fills in the trip home with her own version of the lecture. I don't think she likes maggots.

Tuesday

Ted Martin started calling me 'Maggot' the next day. Before too long, some of the other sheep joined in. It wasn't unusual to hear, "Hey Maggot," called out to me five to six times on the way to class for the next week or two. But eventually, people got sick of that joke and left it alone...except for Ted Martin.

Ted Martin had a permanent mean look on his face. His stocky, muscular build and spiky haircut finished the image, and most kids were scared of him. He was the type of bully that once he targeted you, he never let go. Ted needs a name, and I decide to call him 'Pitbull.' I could see that Pitbull would be an ongoing problem for me. After all, how can I be a cool girl and try to fit in when he keeps calling me Maggot.

Mr. TDH offered to tell Pitbull to back off for me, but I didn't want him to get into a fight and get hurt or in trouble. I should have just told the teachers, but Pitbull was smart and never did it in front of any teachers, and the other kids were too scared to speak against him. It would be hard to prove; it would be my friend's word against him and his friends. I'd have to solve this my way.

Now Pitbull didn't just name-call; he was quite versatile. He indulged in a bit of push and shove, tacks on your chair, throwing your bag into the bushes, taking your hat, and pulling faces, but his specialty was taking your lunch. Daily he would stalk the eating area to select a victim who had a nice sandwich or, even better, a slice of chocolate cake. Pitbull would snatch the food away in a millisecond and laugh as he walked off.

Wednesday

I have hatched my plan to stop Pitbull calling me Maggot and maybe stop him from stealing lunches at the same time. Putting my recent experience with maggots to good use, I decided to create a little maggot farm. I carefully collected a few tasty left-overs and put them into a plastic lunch container with the lid off, and left it in the backyard.

***

The Following Wednesday

After a week, I had a nice colony of maggots, put the lid back on the container, and then took it to school (carefully! I didn't want another bag incident).

That lunchtime, I waited patiently for Pitbull to prowl the eating area. I kept my slice of chocolate cake out of sight until just before the bell went. Then I start telling Gretel and Mr. TDH how lovely Mom's chocolate cake was (I used a loud voice), waving it around in front of them as I spoke.

As soon as I saw Pitbull approaching, I quickly slipped it into the plastic lunch container (you know, the lunch container I prepared at home).

Pitbull reached for me just as the bell went and snatched the container right out of my hands. "Too late, Maggot, I saw your chocolate cake. This will make a nice mid-class snack for me," he sneered as he put the container in his pocket.

Pitbull often liked to keep some of his stolen food in his pockets, and when the teachers weren't looking, he would grab a quick bite. Pitbull sat in the middle of the room, and I was several rows back. Our English teacher, who I preferred to call Mr. Albert because of his frizzy Albert Einstein hairdo, gives a riveting lesson on nouns and verbs.

However, my attention is focused on Pitbull. Halfway through the lesson, I can see Pitbull starting to get restless, and then he reaches into his pocket, and I hear the snap of the lunch box lid being undone. Mr. Albert starts walking around the room as he talks, and Pitbull quickly whips his hand out of his pocket. As I continue to watch, I notice the little white maggots climbing up the side and along the back of his shirt. Soon Pitbull's back is a super highway for maggots as they escape the lunch container, some keep going up and some turnaround and go down, and some just go around in circles.

As Mr. Albert turns back to the board, Pitbull goes for a quick bite of the chocolate cake. Suddenly the room is rocked by the sound of coughing and spluttering as Pitbull realizes that he has a mouth full of chocolate cake and maggots!

The coughing turns to vomiting as Mr. Albert escorts him from the room. Mr. Albert looks like he would like to vomit too. Double win! I don't think Pitbull will be calling me maggot anymore; in fact, I'd be surprised if he ever uses the word maggot again. Hopefully, he also thinks twice before stealing anyone's food again.

We were sent out of class early so that the mess can be removed by the cleaners. Pitbull had to help them. Mrs. She Who Runs The School supervises us as we leave. She stares at me suspiciously, but I just give her a cheeky smile. Problem solved.

Thursday

Recreational Sport – Oh no...

I read the Recreational Sports note, and t said to put your name down for the sport of your choice.

Unfortunately, Recreational Sport will be run on Fridays for six weeks.

There are about six choices of sports, including volleyball, skating, and fishing, but straight away, my attention is grabbed by tenpin bowling. Air-conditioned, a takeaway food counter and music - now that sounds like my kind of sport.

So, I quickly put my name down.

Friday

The first week of tenpin bowling comes up fast, and the supervising teacher is Mr. Eagle. I call him Mr. Eagle because of his bald head, the beady black eyes that just peer into your mind, and the way he moves his head thrust slightly forward. Mr. Eagle swiftly forms us into groups for each alley. I end up in a group of four, which is good because you spend less time waiting. But bad because the group is Gretel, another girl called Sally, Pitbull and me. That is just my bad luck; I can't believe that I managed to get stuck in his group!

Since the maggot food incident, I wouldn't say Pitbull has been nice to me...but carefully neutral around me. Like Mrs. She Who Runs The School, he suspects my involvement with his embarrassing maggot episode. I wouldn't say he is scared of me, just wary.

Pitbull bowls first, of course! He doesn't so much bowl the ball; he hurls the ball down the alley. His run-up is so fast and his arm so powerful...it's a wonder the 10 pins don't shatter.

Then you have Sally, who is quite the opposite. She slowly walks out onto the alley, the ball seems almost too heavy for her, and she nearly drags it along the ground. Sally releases the ball so slowly it just kind of meanders down the alley. It finally reaches the pins but doesn't knock any over; it just comes to a halt resting against them. After a few minutes, one of the staff comes across and moves the ball and tells us to stop being silly and bowl correctly.

Gretel and I both managed to bowl a few balls down, and I've even knocked some pins over. Meanwhile, Pitbull continues his frenzied attacks on the 10 pins sending them flying into the air each time. Eventually, Pitbull can't help himself and starts making little snide comments about how weak we are and how our bowling "sucks." Of course, that annoys me, and on my next turn, I do a much faster run-up and put all my strength into bowling that ball as fast as I can. It does go fast, the fastest I've ever bowled before.

Unfortunately, I let go at the wrong time, and my bowling ball isn't going down the alley but is heading back towards where the others are sitting. With a loud thump, it lands on Pitbull's leg. He gives out an impressive shriek.

I race back to him, apologizing, but he gives me his best mean stare. "You did that on purpose!" he yells at me. "Don't be silly," I reply, "I am not that accurate with my bowling."

While Pitbull limps over for his next go, I race over and buy a soft drink. I get back in time to quickly have my next go, making sure it goes down the alley this time. I sit down with my drink when I see that my five-dollar bill has fallen out of my pocket and it is on the floor at the front of our alley. I race out to grab it as Pitbull selects his ball from the return rack. I'm in such a hurry I spill my drink on the floor. "Wait!" I yell to Pitbull as I go to get a mop to wipe it up.

Pitbull generally doesn't listen to anyone, and he certainly doesn't listen to me. As he goes to have his next bowl, he goes even faster to make up for his limp (from my bowling ball). His feet hit my puddle of soft drink, and Pitbull goes flying in the air. He goes so fast he continues to slide down the alley, and his head hits the 10 pins - a strike actually, well done, Pitbull. The attendant rushes to Pitbull's aid as the rest of the students clap. As Pitbull is helped up the alley to the seats, I tried to apologize again. He just looks at me and says, "Stay away from me!"

Buddy Class – How Cool!

"Everybody listen up," gushes Miss Learning Is Fun. "Today, we have our first meeting with our year one buddy class, and I have paired each one of you with a lovely grade one child. It's your job to be a responsible and sensible mentor. These little girls and boys will be shy and nervous around you big kids, so make sure you are extra nice with lots of warm smiles to make them feel welcome."

Little kids, I love little kids, so cute and adorable. How exciting to be a mentor, a big friend, to be able to reach across the years and offer a helping hand. I know, I know - I'm beginning to sound like my mother. But this is going to be fantastic!

Miss Learning Is Fun walks us down to the year one building in the lower school. That's where we meet the year one teacher, Mrs. Jones, who sounds like Miss Learning Is Fun, magnified ten times. Her enthusiasm is infectious, and the two teachers quickly call out names to match us with a partner.

Gretel gets a cute little girl with pigtails in red bows. Mr. Tall Dark And Handsome gets an adorable little boy with a huge smile. My buddy is called Dean, but he looks more like Dennis the Menace. Short, spiky red hair, a handful of freckles thrown across his face, a temporary snake tattoo on his arm, and displaying a gap-toothed grin or smile (I'm not sure which). "That's an interesting tattoo," I say.

"I like snakes," he replies, "they bite people." I don't know what to say to that, so I say nothing.

Our first buddy task is to color in a picture. With my artistic flair, I'll soon have Dean and me creating a masterpiece.

Except, Dean informs me in his cranky voice with a matching cranky face that he doesn't like coloring and refuses to do the coloring sheet. I followed Miss Learning Is Fun's instructions and gave him my big smile and using my nicest voice, I offered to let him use my connector pens. This works perfectly, and a smile appears on his face.

But my smile fades as Dean quickly puts my pens together to make a Star Wars sword and starts to hit Gretel and Mr. Tall Dark And Handsome, with it. "Stop!" I yell and snatch the pens off him, putting them back on the desk.

Mrs. Learning Is Fun comes rushing over. "Madonna, remember you are a mentor. Raising your voice like that is going to scare your buddy."

I start to explain what he was doing when I realize that Dean is now quietly coloring the sheet. Miss Learning Is Fun gives me an unbelieving look and walks away. Dean just gives me a sly grin and alternates between coloring and sucking and chewing on my pens.

At last, the picture is finished, and I try to retrieve my pens from Dean. I got them all except my favorite pink-colored one that he continues to chew on. I try to yank it from his mouth, but because by now it is covered in slimy grade 1 boy saliva, it slips out of my hands and hits Miss Learning Is Fun in the back of the head.

Great, I get another lecture about being a responsible mentor and threatened with detention.

The second activity involves us reading a simple book while the buddies follow the words with their fingers. It starts well, Dean does an excellent job for the first three pages, but then I noticed his fingers have disappeared from the page.

I look up from the book to see what he's doing. No wonder his fingers aren't following the words. He now has two of his fingers jammed far up his nose. As I watch the fingers reemerge from their mining expedition, they are now covered in green snot! Yuck!

"Hang on, Dean, I'll get you a tissue," I say. No need, Dean sticks his fingers into his mouth and starts chewing into an early lunch.

I promptly turn around and vomit onto the reading book.

As Miss Learning Is Fun leads me down to the sick bay, she says, "Now I know why you were not a good mentor. You must be coming down with something." "I know you'll do a fantastic job next week when you get to work with Dean again."

Miss Learning Is Fun thinks my groaning is because I feel sick, so she pats me on the shoulder.

Next week for buddy time, I think I'll bring a set of handcuffs and a bottle of disinfectant!

Dad's Surprise

I arrive home from school ready to kick back, grab a snack and maybe watch a little TV. My mellow mood is lost when I walk in and find Dad waiting for me with that smile on his face. You know that smile, the one your parents have when they've done something that they think is marvelous, and in reality, it's your worst nightmare.

He is hiding something behind his back. He brings his hands to the front, revealing a hideous yellow shirt with a number on the back and some matching long black and yellow socks. I stare vacantly, still not getting it, when Dad announces he has signed me up for soccer.

The news only gets better! My first training session is on this afternoon. Now don't get me wrong, I think sport is great to watch. I know playing sport helps you to be fit and healthy, and sometimes I jog, but my coordination with ball sports isn't good. This is maybe because I have been very good at avoiding ball sports. It is surprising how easy it is to fake an injury or illness with a bit of Internet research.

We arrive at the soccer fields. Dad takes me across and introduces me to the coach, Mr. Cameron. Mr. Cameron introduces me to the rest of the team, about 14 kids. I'm glad to see the team includes four other girls. Mr. Cameron tells me to call him Coach, as that is what everybody else calls him. I must admit he is not what I expected, a towering mass of muscle yelling at the players. Coach isn't overly tall but looks fit; he seems to have a permanent smile on his face and a calm, soft voice.

Coach tells us to all grab a soccer ball and jog around the field as a warm-up. I'm keen to make a good impression, so I quickly grab a ball and tuck it under my arm and take off first. I run hard, and I'm the first back to the coach.

He smiles at me and says, "Madonna, when I said grab a ball, I meant to get a ball and dribble it with your feet around the field. This is soccer. We don't run and carry the ball." He told me to look at the others. I watched the rest of the team kicking the ball along as they run.

Great first impression...how embarrassing!

We do lots more running and dribbling the ball and some passing with partners.

Finally, the coach calls us in for the last activity. He lines some balls up in front of the goal and instructs us to give one strong kick into the goal. I wisely head to the back of the line so I can watch and learn. The first few boys kick the ball straight into the goal, and a few kick it too hard and send it way over the top of the goal. The other girls each kick it into the goal but not quite as hard as the boys. What a relief. This doesn't look too difficult at all.

Then it is my turn. I get a good run-up and swing my right leg as powerfully as I can. Stand clear everyone, I think, here comes a Madonna missile. No missile, in fact, the ball doesn't even move. My kick is a big air swing. I don't even touch the ball, but I do overbalance and fall flat on my bottom.

The whole team erupts in laughter, but the coach quickly tells them to stop. "Have another go Madonna," he urges, "but this time come in a bit more slowly."

I go back to the starting point and try again. This time I do connect with the ball. Unfortunately, my boot just seems to slide off the side of the ball. The ball rolls to the left about a body length before stopping.

This time the team is more controlled and doesn't burst into 'loud' laughter. I can still see some of their looks, as they try to hold their laughter in.

When the training session ends, the coach calls me over. Perhaps I'll be saved, and he'll dump me from the team.

No such luck. He gives me a friendly smile and a few more tips. "One more thing Madonna, those shin pads are supposed to be worn under your socks and not on top of them."

I hope he thinks my face is red from all the running around…not from the embarrassment of being such a kook.

Oh, Boris!!!!

Boris the Bear sits at my student desk in my bedroom, staring at me with those sad brown eyes. One eye is dangling down his cheek by a single thread. One ear is ripped off, a gaping hole in his stomach is leaking polyester stuffing, and his left foot is wet and fraying. A black tire tread mark is across his back. I've let everyone in my class down; they are all going to be so disappointed.

OOPS! REWIND! You will want to know how poor Boris the bear ended up like this. Who is Boris the Bear? Well, he is the property of Miss Learning Is Fun. She has had Boris since she was a little girl (which must be a very long time ago – she has to be at least 30).

Anyway, Miss Learning Is Fun had this great idea to help us with our writing. We each get to take Boris the Bear home and take photos of him in different situations. Then we bring them to school, and the class can choose from one of the photos to write a story. It's something a bit different, and everyone enjoys taking Boris home and trying to outdo each other in finding unusual places to photograph Boris.

That's when I had my great idea…I'd take Boris to the zoo and get some photos of him with a real bear.

On Saturday, I asked Mr. TDH and Gretel to come with me to the zoo. I borrowed Mom's camera, and off we go. We decide to catch the bus to the zoo, and we feel pretty grown up as we walked down to the bus stop. That is until I noticed little kids and adults giving me funny looks. You see, Boris the Bear is too big to fit into my bag, so I'm carrying Boris in my arms like a baby. I guess a girl my age carrying a bear in public isn't terribly cool.

I try and stick Boris under my jumper, but this looks even stranger, and he keeps falling out. Brain wave hits, I tuck Boris under my belt at my back, and my sweatshirt covers him. Problem solved, and we quickly reach the bus stop. We only wait a few minutes before the bus arrives, and we hop on. We choose the back seat, and before I sit down…I reach back to remove Boris. Gone!!! Boris must have fallen out as I climbed onto the bus. In a panic, I look out the back window as the bus pulls away. I spot Boris lying on the road just before the bus stop. Quickly we race to the front of the bus and ask the driver to stop and let us off. He says he can't let us off until the next official stop.

Five minutes later (okay – maybe only 2) and several kilometers (or a few hundred meters) further away, we finally get off the bus. We run back, and finally, the original bus stop is insight, and I can still see Boris on the road. With relief, I see that he appears unmarked until I look at his back and see the bus tire tread mark right across the middle. I tried to brush it off, but it only slightly smudges. It is a mix of oil and road grime, no way it's coming off.

Mr. TDH, bless his heart, says, "Don't worry, Madonna, it won't show up in the photos. You'll only see the front of Boris." I realize he is right; I can worry about cleaning it off later.

Finally, we get to the zoo, and all of us get distracted for a while looking at all the different animals. The tiger enclosure is fantastic with big glass panels (that are really thick – I hope), so you can see the tigers clearly. Gretel suggests we just get photos of Boris with the Tigers in the background. But no, I insist on a bear photo, and a check on the zoo map reveals a grizzly bear enclosure not far from where we are.

We quickly arrived at the grizzly bear enclosure, but we are disappointed to find it doesn't have glass viewing walls.

Instead, it has a high mesh wall that keeps us back from the steel bars of the main enclosure area. The mesh fence is going to be super hard to take pictures through, but then we spy a viewing platform that overlooks the enclosure, and this will give us a clear picture above the mesh fence. I get Mr. TDH to hold Boris up with the enclosure in the background. But the real bear is too close to the front of the enclosure, and I can't fit both the stuffed bear and the real bear in the photo.

I instruct Mr. TDH to hold Boris the Bear out over the fence as far as possible and lower. Mr. TDH looks a bit nervous, but I tell him not to worry. But his hand is in the photo, so I ask him just to hold Boris by the tip of his ear. Mr. TDH reaches out and down, and I start to line up the perfect shot. The grizzly bear lets out a huge roar and slams against the fence with a tremendous rattle. As he rips his hand back, Boris slips from his fingers, falls onto the top of the main fence, and bounces into the bear enclosure.

Mr. TDH shrieks, I shriek louder, Gretel shakes her head. I pass Gretel the camera and race down to the ground level, closely followed by Mr. TDH. I can't see Boris in the enclosure; maybe he bounced back out. No! There he is in the real bear's paws! Grizzly lifted Boris to his mouth and grabbed his left ear with his teeth. I hear a ripping noise as the ear is ripped from Boris's head. Boris falls to the ground, and the bear pounces on him again. His jaw grasps Boris around the stomach, bits of stuffing go flying everywhere. The bear shakes Boris again and drops him to the ground.

The grizzly has a wonderful game with our class bear. He grabs Boris again, this time by the left foot, and shakes his head from side to side wildly. Boris slips from the bear's mouth and goes flying. He lands halfway between the main bars of the enclosure and the mesh fence.

I race over and reach under the bottom of the mesh fence to try to get Boris. Grizzly does the same thing from his side of the enclosure. Fortunately, the grizzlies' paw is too wide to get through the bars on the fence. But he doesn't give up and tries to dig under the fence to get to Boris. Mr. TDH stretches his arm under the fence. For one horrible moment, Mr. TDH's hand touches one of the grizzly's paws. He snatches his hand back, dragging Boris back. As the grizzly roars in frustration, we pull Boris out from under the fence.

We looked at each other, still a bit in shock, and I realize not only is he tall, dark, and handsome, but he's also my hero. Boris is torn and tattered, but at least I have him back. Then Gretel comes charging down from the viewing platform with a great big grin on her face. "I got the best photos ever," she beams.

So that's why I'm sitting here in my bedroom with poor Boris the Bear looking so tattered and torn. I feel so bad; Miss Learning Is Fun will be so upset when she sees her childhood bear. The other kids in the class have grown so attached to Boris as well. I've let everyone down, but I'll have to face the music and go and see Miss Learning Is Fun first thing in the morning.

I arrive at school early and hurry to Miss Learning Is Fun's room. As would be expected, she's already setting up her class for the day's learning. She greets me with a smile, and I blurt out how sorry I am for ruining her bear as I hold Boris out to her. Her face displays shock as her eyes take in the terrible damage Boris has suffered.

Then she looks back at me and smiles. "Don't worry, Madonna," she says, "come into my office."

I followed her in and watch in amazement as she opens a cupboard door to reveal three other immaculate Boris the

Bears sitting inside. She pulls out one and replaces it with the tattered bear I have returned. "You see, Madonna, every year one or two Boris the Bears don't survive the photo sessions, so I always keep some spares," smiles Miss Learning Is Fun. "But I thought Boris the Bear was your favorite childhood toy."

"Yes, Madonna, he was, but my Boris the bear is a beautiful black and white panda bear, so no way was I letting a bunch of crazy kids put him in harm's way. "The Boris legend encourages the kids to take more care of the bear. Although, obviously not in your case. Gretel has emailed me your photos, and I must say they are the best ever. Well done, Madonna, and remember the extra bears have to remain our little secret."

The Soccer Game

I sit bolt upright in bed as Dad's booming voice sings out, "We are the champions." "Come up, Madonna, game day! Time to get up!" continues Dad.

Today is the day of my first soccer game. I'm glad Dad is excited because I'm terrified. I get dressed, and on the way to the field, Dad gives me a pregame pep talk. "Make every kick count, be first to the ball, push-up when you're defending," and a whole lot of other stuff which made no sense to me at all.

On arriving at the field, I jog over to join the others gathering around the coach. I notice the other team at the opposite end of the field. They look like they had cornflakes and steroids for breakfast. A few of my teammates also look nervously at our opponents.

The coach picks up on our nervous looks and admits the other team is big, fast, and very good. He also reminds us that winning isn't everything and the important thing is to play our best and enjoy the game. I love our coach.

"Remember," he says, "you didn't join the team to win games. You joined because you like playing soccer."

Hang on; I only joined because Dad signed me up. Anyway, knowing that the coach isn't going to be upset with us if we lose takes some of the nerves away.

Coach shows us his game plan and assigns us playing positions. He makes me a left midfielder. When I ask which left, he looks at me strangely for a while, then walks me to the other side of the field and shows me where to stand.

Soon the referee blows his whistle, and we run onto the field and shake hands with the other team. So far...so good. I take my position, and while waiting for the game to start, I glance at the sideline.

Great news, standing alongside Dad and Mom are Gretel and Mr. TDH. Mom must have brought them along to watch me play. Dad spots me looking and gives a booming, "Go, Madonna!" How embarrassing!

The referee blows the whistle, and the game starts. I stand in my position and watch as the other team constantly attacks down the opposite side, scoring several goals. So far, the ball has come nowhere near me but rolls past just out of my reach. That happened another three times, and each time I watch it roll past. I'm beginning to wonder if the coach told me to stand in the wrong spot. Finally, the referee signals halftime, and we jog off the field for a drink.

Coach calls me aside, "Madonna," he patiently explains, "when I showed you where to stand, I didn't mean you couldn't move. That's where to stand at the start of the game. You can move around to get the ball when it comes near your side of the field."

"Okay," I reply, as my face turns a beetroot red color.

Soon half time is over, and we are called back onto the field. Dad starts giving some cheerleader type calls, "M.A.D.O.N.N.A – Go, Madonna!" He uses his earsplitting loudest possible voice.

I notice that one of the attacking forwards in the other team is a very athletic looking girl with pigtails. As she sprints past me for the third time, I comment that I like her hair. She looks at me in confusion and stumbles into me, and trips over.

The referee blows the whistle and gives me a yellow card (a warning of rough play, and if I get another one, it becomes a red card, and I get kicked out of the game). I tried to explain that I didn't trip her, but he waves me away. I offer my hand to help the girl to her feet and notice she is wearing a lovely bright pink mouthguard. I remind myself to get one of those for the next game.

Meanwhile, Mr. Boom Boom (my Dad) is going ballistic over the referee giving me the yellow card until Mom tells him to be quiet.

The game recommences, and the other team scores another goal from the free kick.

On the kickoff, the ball somehow ends up at my feet. Remembering everything my coach has taught me, I kick it as hard as possible, and it goes flying down the field.

Well, if I thought Dad had been loud before, now it was on the 10 out of 10 scale. "Go, Madonna, that's my daughter!" And then he starts the Madonna chant again.

Suddenly the referee blows his whistle to stop the game and strides angrily over to my Dad on the sideline. I can't hear everything the referee says, but the main point is that Dad has to be quiet because the players can't hear his whistle and his instructions. "Be quiet or leave the grounds!" yells the referee.

That's my Dad...how embarrassing. I notice that Mom, Gretel, and Mr. TDH have all shuffled along a bit from my Dad.

The game restarts, and I get a few more kicks, and dad manages to stay reasonably quiet. The girl with the pigtails gets past me several times to score more goals. The coach tells one of the other players, Mary, to drop back to help me to defend against her attacking runs.

Miss Piggy Tails starts another run aiming to get past me, but Mary shoulder charges her, and this sends her crashing to the ground. Mary heads off with the ball.

As everyone else heads off in pursuit of the ball, I noticed that Miss Piggy Tails hasn't got back up and is lying quite still on the ground. I rush over to her and squat down to check on her. She is going blue in the face and making strange noises.

By now, the referee has noticed and has stopped the game and rushes over. The referee and the rest of the team have gathered around. I see half her lovely pink mouth guard lying next to her head. Then it dawns on me that she is choking. I open her mouth and reach in and feel around. My fingers brush against the other end of the mouthguard, so I grab it and try to pull it out, but it's stuck firmly in her throat, I pull harder, and it pops out of her mouth.

Miss Piggy Tails gives a giant gasp and sits up, sucking in air in huge gulps.

Just then, the paramedics arrive. They quickly check her over, and the referee tells them what I did. One of the paramedics turns to me and says, "Well done, young lady, you saved her life."

Some of the other players run back to their parents on the sideline. I stand in shock, watching Miss Piggy Tails talking to the paramedics. She is helped off, and I slowly walk over to my family.

As I approach the sideline, the spectators from both teams start to clap. Dad's voice booms out, "Three cheers for Madonna!" As the cheers die down, I reach Mom and Dad. They each give me a big cuddle and a kiss. People gather around and pat me on the back.

Then Gretel gives me a big hug and whispers, "You are fantastic." Mr. TDH also hugs me and tells me that I'm a hero. Me... a hero! Is this a dream? I LOVE SOCCER! And I LOVE my new school!

BOOK 3

MEET THE COUSINS

Wednesday – New Year's Eve

Boom, another flash rips apart the dark of the night sky. The sounds are deafening, and the exploding colors sear your eyeballs. My heart pounds like a drum in my chest while my companion lies under my bed. His tongue hangs out of his mouth as he pants loudly. Finally, the explosions finish. That's it, the end, Madonna Bull (that's me) has officially survived another year.

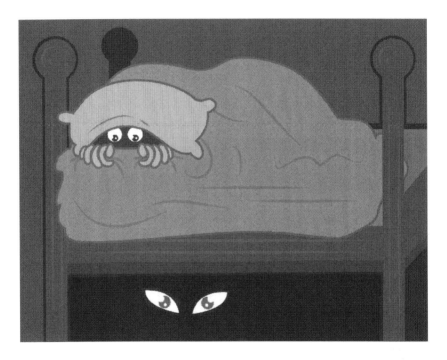

A bit embarrassing greeting the start of a new year hiding under the blankets, but I've always found the fireworks on New Year's Eve scary. So, when Dad, I call him Mr. Boom Boom because of his ear-destroying loud voice, bought some fireworks to put on his own private display, I knew I was in for a wild night. (A new reason to call him Mr. Boom Boom!)

Fortunately, I'm not the only one in the family scared of fireworks, so is Tyson, our family's pet Great Dane. Tyson joined me when I snuck back upstairs and hid in my bedroom. Girl and dog turned into chickens by a few fireworks.

I'm a little sad the year is over; I've had such a great year. I moved to Harper Valley School, made some great friends like Gretel and the dreamy Richard Jones, or as I call him, Mr. Tall Dark and Handsome. My Mom and Dad got back together after a brief separation, and I learned to play soccer.

As silence descends the house, a beaming Mr. Boom Boom calls us all together. "I've got some exciting news," he starts. When my Dad is enthusiastic, his voice gets even louder! "We're going on a holiday to Australia to meet your Uncle Jim, Aunty Jill, and your two cousins."

AUSTRALIA – wow, for once, Dad is on a winner. Australia sounds so exciting! But Uncle Jim and Aunty Jill are just a mystery to me. Aunty Jill is Dad's sister. I've only met her once before when she visited us for a week. I was only young, but from memory, she was a female version of Dad…booming voice and tall and imposing like Dad. I've never met Uncle Jim or their two children, my cousins. This certainly sounds like an interesting trip.

When Dad makes a decision, he acts on it fast! "We leave in TWO days!" he announces.

Friday

The house is frantic as we plan and pack. I carefully pack all my best clothes into two bags before Mom burst into the room to help me. I call her Mrs. Absolutely Positive because she always sees the positive side of things. She's great, and I love her so much, but sometimes a kid can only take so much positivity!

This trip seems to be stressing Mom out.

I don't get her normal *everything will be fine* smile. Instead, I get, "You can't take that much luggage," yell. "One bag!"

Just call me one bag Madonna. Sadly, I cut back my clothes to one bag, but then I have a brainwave...on the day we leave. I'll just wear more than one outfit, brilliant!

Saturday

On the morning we leave, we have to drop Tyson at the *Doggie Vacation Resort*. It doesn't look like a resort to me! I don't think it looks like a resort to Tyson either! I feel sad to leave Tyson, but a Great Dane on a plane just isn't going to work for anyone. It's my job to lead him into the resort. He looks at me with those big puppy dog eyes, and I feel like a traitor. I give Tyson one of his favorite dog biscuits and a big cuddle. Dad and I both have tears in our eyes as we leave, but I know Tyson will be safe, and we'll see him soon.

I've managed to squirm into 3 tops, but they are all different colors and styles, and it looks pretty silly. I put a long-sleeved white shirt over the top of them. I even manage to get two pairs of long pants on too. Yes, I move very stiffly. Yes, I look like an overinflated version of myself. But at least some of my favorite clothes from my second bag will get to come on holiday with me.

We arrive at the airport, and after about an hour, we finally are all checked in and waiting to get on the plane. The call is made to board the plane, and together we head up the gangway to the plane door. With all those clothes on, I have a definite waddle going on. I can barely keep up with my parents, and I overhear Dad whisper to my Mom, "I think we had better cut down on treats for Maddi."

At the entrance to the plane awaits the beautiful, smiling hostess, perfect hair, perfect uniform, and of course…a perfect smile. I think her name is obvious – Miss Perfect! That's until I reach the entrance, then the perfect smile slips into an "oh" of surprise and then a quiet laugh. "Well, with a shirt like that, you won't have to worry about spilling your food on yourself," the perfect girl in the perfect uniform laughs. Miss Perfect is quite rude.

Then I follow her eyes and look down at my shirt. Tyson! Great Danes are incredible dogs, big legs, big tails, big heads, and very big mouths that unfortunately make very big spit messes. That goodbye cuddle with Tyson has left my shirt covered in a lovely mix of dog spit, dog hair, and a half-chewed dog biscuit.

I ask Mom and Dad why they didn't tell me. They just smile and reply that we didn't have time to go back to get another shirt. I'm wearing three other shirts! But they didn't know that, and I couldn't tell them that I had all those clothes on (that I was told NOT to bring). I guess that's why they say…honesty is the best policy.

Once we take off, Miss Perfect redeems herself by bringing a hot wet towel and helping me to clean up my shirt.

Sometimes I think my family is a little strange, but as I sit in my seat on the plane, I realize I'm definitely right. There's my Mom on the other side of the aisle listening to some music with those headphones they provide on the plane. It seems harmless enough until she starts to sing along with the song out loud. Mom has many amazing talents.

Unfortunately, singing isn't one of them! Her badly off-tone voice screeches out as she happily sings along with the range of rock songs, but my personal favorite is Mom's version of We Will Rock You.

It's my favorite because the ever-smiling Miss Perfect has forgotten her perfect smile as she taps Mom on the arm to get her attention. "Excuse me, can we please ask you to stop singing," she asks in her pleasant voice.

"What!" yells Mom, "speak up. I can't hear you!" Isn't it funny when people with headphones on can't hear you…they seem to forget they can just take them off, and they yell as if everyone else can't hear?

Miss Perfect's perfection is slipping away. She yanks the headphones off Mom's head and snarls, "Can you please stop that awful singing? You are annoying the whole plane."

That's when my Mom – Mrs. Absolutely Positive – lives up to her name. "Oh, sorry dear, well, at least I gave everyone something to talk about. These long plane trips can be so boring," she replies with a smile and a wink.

Miss Perfect tries to return the smile, but not with much warmth, and I notice she keeps the headphones in her hand as she walks away down the aisle.

I turn to Dad to smile at him about the "singing" incident, but he has fallen asleep. Oh NO, I cringe. I call Dad - Mr. Boom Boom because of his earth-shattering voice…but when Dad falls asleep, his ability to make enormous noises continues. Dad's snoring is just beginning, but from experience, I know it will only grow in volume as he goes into a deeper sleep.

I decide to wake him up, but I don't want him to know it was me, or he'll be grumpy all flight. I try giving him a nudge with my elbow, but he doesn't even quiver. I flick his ear with my finger, he turns his head, but there is no sign of awakening. The snoring starts to get louder. Finally, in desperation, I lift his eyelid revealing a blood-shot eye slightly rolled back in his head. Gross! But he is still fast asleep.

There is only one thing to do, give up! I take out my set of headphones, crank up the volume and start to enjoy the music. I tap the beat to the music on the armrest of the chair…but take care NOT to sing. I don't want to sound like my mother.

I'm really relaxed and enjoying the music with my chair back and my eyes closed when I feel a very insistent tapping on my arm. My eyes spring open to find Miss Perfect kneeling down in the aisle next to my seat. "Excuse me," she says, "is that your father making that dreadful noise? Is he okay, or is this some kind of medical emergency?"

"Yes, he's my father," I reply.

Mom leans across the aisle and butts in, "He's my husband too."

"Of course, he is," replies Miss Perfect, "I should have realized," she says in a strange tone of voice. I tell her that Dad is okay; he is just a loud snorer.

"Well, dear, you'll just have to wake him up. He is disturbing the whole plane," she quietly snaps. I'm beginning to think she doesn't like our family.

I try the tap on the arm, the shake of the shoulder, even the elbow in the ribs, but Dad barely stirs. He's like a bear in hibernation for the winter.

That's when I get my brilliant idea. I've got one of those plastic drinking cups that they serve your drinks in on the plane. I've finished the drink, but the ice cubes are still in the cup. Dad is still thundering away; Miss Perfect is at the other end of the aisle, glaring at us and coming our way.

Desperate times call for desperate measures! I pull Dad's shirt out from his neck and tip the ice cubes down the front of his shirt. That works! Dad comes awake with a bellow, tries to jump up from his seat, but the belt jerks him back down. He crazily starts trying to flick the ice out from his shirt, and this sends the ice cubes flying in all directions.

Some of the flying ice missiles hit human targets, the passengers in front of us! Some even manage to slip down their shirt and dress fronts, and before you know it, four other people are jumping up in their seats, making strange noises as the ice cubes slide down against their skin.

Mom starts laughing hysterically! Dad joins in with his booming laugh, and I just try to shrink into the chair.

Miss Perfect comes storming down the aisle. With her perfectly false smile, she quietly snarls, "Keep the noise down, or I'll leave the **Keep Seatbelts Fastened** sign on for the whole flight."

Yes, that's my family, they have turned Miss Perfect into a rabid monster, and we are only halfway through the flight. Mom and Dad wink at me, and we all sit back and settle down, just like a "normal" family.

Finally, the flight arrives in Sydney. The view from the plane was incredible! I whip out my Polaroid camera and take my first photo of Australia.

Sunday (Australian time)

We collect our hand luggage and shuffle along the aisle.
There is no sight
of Miss Perfect as we depart the plane, after dealing with our
family, she is probably busy looking for another
job…something more relaxing like being a crocodile handler
or a test crash dummy!

After we get through customs, we head into the main part of
the airport to meet up with our relatives. The airport is
FULL of people, and we gaze around looking for Aunty Jill
when suddenly I hear this booming female voice, "Hey
Bully, I'm over here!" It's Dad's sister, Aunty Jill. Oh my
gosh, she sounds just like Dad, only a bit more girly – scary!

Aunty Jill is very different from my Mom; her face is very
made-up with copious amounts of make-up and very short
blonde hair that is so stiff it doesn't move. Not even a single
hair!

Aunty Jill herds us out to the car park, and we jump into her
big 4-wheel drive. She explains that Uncle Jim and our two
cousins, Jenny and Jack, are waiting at the units where we
are staying. We'll be there for a couple of days before we
head north up the coastline.

Jill, Jim, Jenny, and Jack…what is it with this family…with
all those J names. I've only met Aunty Jill once before when I
was very young, so I'm watching and listening to her
carefully, to get an impression of what she's like. I've got one
word that describes her quite well. Bossy! And even in the
wind, her hair does not move at all.

A lot of her sentences start with…you should. You should go to bed early tonight. You should get something to eat at the Chinese restaurant over the road from the units. You should go to the Sydney Bridge Walk.

Mom mentions that she would like to visit Bondi Beach because it looks so beautiful. Mom has seen a show about Bondi, and it is on her "to do" list.

"You shouldn't worry about going to Bondi," booms Aunty Jill, "seen one beach, and you've seen them all, you'll see plenty of beaches on our road trip." Mom gives her a strained smile. Come on, Mrs. Absolutely Positive, you can do better than that!

When we go up to the units, we find that although they are separate units, they have a door that is unlocked and lets you go from one unit to the other. We are quickly introduced to Uncle Jim. He is tall, sun-tanned, and seems quite nice, not quite as "intense" as his wife.

I also get to meet my cousins, Jenny and Jack. Jenny is the same age as me, while Jack is about three years younger.

Of course, Aunty Jill says, "**You should** get to know each other." She shuffles us into the other unit. Awkward!!!! For what seems like a VERY long moment, we stare at each other. Jenny is stunningly beautiful with brown eyes and brown hair that falls to the middle of her back and whiter than white teeth.

Jack looks very different with reddish sandy-colored hair.

We exchange a few strained greetings as we eye each other up and down. "Your hair is so beautiful," I blurt out to Jenny. "I know," she replies.

"And you're so cute," I continue to Jack. "Yes," he replies.

Okay, mental note, modesty isn't a highly valued quality in this family. Jenny re-enforces this idea with her next statement, "I have an IQ of 148 and had to skip two-year levels at school because I'm so smart. Also, I've been Dux every year that I've attended school."

"That's um, nice," I reply while thinking how Brains will be a great nickname for Jenny. "How about you, Jack?" I ask, "I suppose you are in your final year about to graduate as a doctor," I continue sarcastically.

"Of course not!" snaps Brains, "he takes after Dad. I'm the brainy one in the family." Then she spends the next ten minutes quizzing me on a mix of questions about Math, English, and Science stuff that I have never heard of.

124

We have just established that Brains is a genius, and I'm NOT when Mom comes in to take us all to lunch. Thanks for the SAVE Mom!!!

After lunch, Brains and I are told by Mrs. Bossy, "You should take Jack up to the rooftop garden and admire the view."

The rooftop is fantastic; the view of the harbor is beautiful! The bridge over the river is huge and very high. Along the top of the bridge, I can see little figures that look like they're moving. When I ask what's that on top of the bridge, Jack tells me that it's people doing the bridge walk. "It's going to be so much fun when we do it tomorrow," he gushes.

I feel a moment of panic, and I hope that "we" doesn't include me! Anyway, it isn't until tomorrow; I'll have plenty of time to think of an excuse not to go.

I then decide to go and get my camera from the unit so I can take some photos. I leave the other two on the roof and head for the lift. I press the button and wait and wait and wait! Then I see the door leading to the stairway. It's only a 10-storey building, and our unit is on the 8th floor. I decide to take the stairs rather than wait for the lift. I hurriedly rush into the stairwell and get down about five steps before I hear the heavy metal stairway door clang shut. I get a terrible feeling as I walk back to the door and try the handle…LOCKED!

Uh oh! I try knocking, but the door is so thick I hardly make any noise. No noise…no way Brains and Jack are going to hear me. I decide to walk down the stairs to the next floor and hope the door isn't locked — three flights further down and still no unlocked doors.

Now I'm getting worried. Each floor further down seems to be getting darker, dirtier, and scarier with graffiti on the walls. No one knows where I am and if I can't find a way out, who knows how long I'll be stuck in here. I think I'm on the third floor, and my legs are on fire from walking down all those flights of stairs when I finally find an unlocked door.

With a loud squeal, the door opens into a large office. It's Sunday, so nobody is there, but luckily for me, there are some lights on, so I can see where I'm going.

At the far side of the room, I can see a lift door that I head straight for. Halfway there, I have an awful thought, what if the office has some type of motion sensor, and I set off an alarm. I freeze. I remember seeing a spy film where the spy crawled along the floor underneath the beams of the motion sensors. I'll look really silly, but who cares? Nobody will see. I drop down to the carpet and start to crawl to the lift.

Then a thought stops me again. Security cameras! I pull my shirt over my head and continue to crawl to the lift. Crawling is SO much slower than walking, and I'm getting carpet burns on my knees and elbows. However, it is better than risking setting off an alarm and getting arrested.

I reach the lift and pray that it doesn't need a special card to make it open and work. It doesn't, and I finally relax as it starts the climb to the 8th floor. I forget about going back up to the roof with my camera, and instead, I grab some ice from the fridge for my carpet burns. When Mom asks me what happened, I decide that admitting to being trapped in the stairwell is just way too embarrassing, so I tell her that I tripped coming out of the lift.

After dinner, Mrs. Bossy (Aunty Jill) decides we should all go out and get some ice cream for dessert. My legs are still killing me, so I use sore knees as an excuse not to go.

As the rest of the family leaves the unit, the news comes on. It doesn't matter where you live in the world; the news is BORING! And then, the following story starts; it is about a mysterious burglar who broke into an office building in a high-rise resort building in Sydney.

They show some poor-quality black and white video of someone crawling along the floor with a shirt pulled over their head. I stopped breathing. Sweat poured out of my hands.

The policeman was talking (focus Maddi – what is he saying!). "...nothing has been stolen. At this stage, we think the suspect is a young teenager, and it may be a kid's prank, but we are continuing our investigation."

Phew, I breathe a sigh of relief. Thank goodness the rest of the family is downstairs getting ice cream! I quickly race into my bedroom and change my clothes. They go to the bottom of my bag, and that is where they will stay until we get home! Close call!!!!

Monday

The following day my peaceful sleep is shattered by the booming sound of Mrs. Bossy's voice, calling rise and shine. I try to ignore her as I figure she must be talking to the sun as it is still dark, and the sun hasn't risen yet. But as the blanket is ripped off me, I realize I'm included. As the whole family assembles in the pre-dawn darkness, Mrs. Bossy starts reading off a list she has made.

Mrs. Bossy likes to make lists!

4.45 leave for bridge

5.00 commence bridge walk

7.00 finish bridge walk

7.05 breakfast

7.15 walk to ferry terminal

8.00 Catch Manly Ferry

How can her hair be perfect at 4:30am!!!!!

4:45 am leave for the bridge
5:00 am commence bridge walk
7:00 am finish bridge walk
7:05 am breakfast
7:15 am walk to Ferry Terminal
8:00 am catch the ferry to Manly
and so on…

True to her list, we are at the base of the bridge at 5:00 am, getting ready for the walk in the pre-dawn darkness.

Dad looks like he is sleepwalking, his eyes are almost closed, and his yawns are so big I can see his tonsils! Mr. Boom Boom is very quiet. He doesn't normally get up until at least 7 am! I take after my Dad; I don't do mornings well.

While my Mom, Mrs. Absolutely Positive, is living up to her name. "How exciting, we'll be able to watch the sunrise from the bridge." She is all perky and excited.

Before we can start the bridge walk, we have to listen to a safety talk. My fear of heights wakes me up instantly, and I carefully listen. I feel a bit more relaxed knowing we each are clipped onto a safety rail for the whole walk.

Then we are each given a set of brown overalls to put over our clothes. Apparently, bridge walkers have no fashion sense.

Finally, we get going, and at the start, it is okay. We walk in a line, and as we come onto the metal walkway that leads to the top of the bridge, our guides clip our safety lines on. The higher we climb, the worse I feel. I'm trembling so much I can barely make my feet move as we reach the very top of the bridge.

Mom and Dad raved about the view, and I must admit…when I stop chanting – "don't look down, don't look down" – and I take a peek, it is spectacular! But a quick look down sends my head spinning!

Did I mention the wind? It's blowing a gale, and the higher we go, the windier it becomes. As Uncle Jim said, "It's windy enough to blow the fleas off a dog." This must be some strange Aussie saying. ☺

Then Mom decides to take a photo of Dad and me. Brown overalls, pale freezing, and sick-looking face, and my hair is a tangle of knots, let's say not one of my best photos!

Mom shows me how she has loaded it onto her Facebook page. "I tagged you, Maddi, so all your friends can see what a great time you are having," she says in a proud voice.

"Thanks, Mom," I reply. I'll get rid of the tag when we get back to the unit.

We continue the walk and finally reach the ground on the other side. I maintain some coolness and stop myself from getting down and kissing the ground. I smile and nod as Brains and Jack go on and on about how amazing the walk was.

We follow Mrs. Bossy's timetable and go to breakfast. I have yummy bacon and eggs, and then I eat half of Mom's pancakes as she is too full. The only downside to breakfast is surviving another of Brain's pop quizzes; she just wants to make sure that I remember that she is a genius.

Then we walk down to the Ferry Terminal. I have no idea what a ferry is. In my early morning haze, I am imagining little fairies flying around, you know, like the tooth fairy. But a ferry is a large old wooden boat.

We quickly board the old boat, and it sets off across the harbor for Manly beach. As we chug along, a new streamline hydrofoil boat speeds past us.

"That's one of the newer boats," scoffed Mrs. Bossy, "they have absolutely no character, and you can't feel the movement of the ocean beneath you." It looks pretty nice to me!

As a surprise, our ferry stops at Luna Park first. Luna Park is an old amusement park with some old-style rides.

We have a lot of fun there; even Brains seems to smile a bit more…after she explains to me how centripetal force worked. Ho Hum!

that's me and Brains

My all time FAVORITE ride!
It is called the **WILD MOUSE!** ☺

Just before we leave to go back on the ferry, I buy some cotton candy (they call it fairy floss here). It was so yum; I finished it off quickly. I can beat Brains at some things!

As the ferry heads across the bay, we hit a few waves, and my stomach begins to churn. As the trip goes on, my stomach grows worse and worse. I start to look for the toilet just in case. I find it! It is just behind the 'Out of Order sign. Oh no, the rocking of the boat is getting worse, as is the rumbling of my stomach. The wind I felt up on the bridge was nearly as strong down here on the water. Things in my stomach department are now getting desperate. I wish I hadn't eaten so much for breakfast or all that cotton candy.

I looked around for Mom and saw that she and Mrs. Bossy are standing at the railing at the front of the boat. I race over to Mom and squeeze in between her and Mrs. Bossy.

Too late! As I start to tell Mom that I think I am going to be sick, I feel a surge of vomit come into my throat. I do the only thing I could do and lean over the railing, letting it erupt out of my mouth. The strange things you notice in situations like these, as the vomit spews from my mouth, I admire its pretty pink color.

On a less windy day, it would have been fine, going over the side of the boat into the water below, but not today. That wind is so strong. So strong that it blows the pink-colored vomit back onboard. Some flecks hit my face, but the vast majority flies back straight into Mrs. Bossy's face. As bits of my breakfast drip off her face, I can't help but think that her makeup and hairdo are ruined for the day.

Mom wipes Mrs. Bossy's face with some tissues as best she can. With her face devoid of makeup and her hair a tangled mess of curls, Mrs. Bossy looks very different. She wants to go home, but Uncle Jim pats her on the back, "Don't worry. She'll be right, mate." Another Aussie saying???

We get off at Manly and have a lovely lunch — I don't feel sick once I get off the ferry. Uncle Jim buys some ginger candy for me to chew so I won't get sick on the return trip. The beach looks beautiful, and we have fun splashing in the shallows. On the return ferry trip, Mrs. Bossy stays well away from me.

It's a bit embarrassing to talk about, but since we've arrived in Sydney, my toilet trips have been ahh — difficult.

I finally tell Mom, and she explains that sometimes when you travel and eat food you're not used to, your bowels can get clogged up.

She buys me a bag of prunes and says if I eat some of them, it should help me. If a few prunes help, the whole bag should fix me straight away!

Maybe Brains isn't the only genius after all.

Tuesday

Today we leave Sydney to head up north along the coast. Mom and Dad have hired a small car to go in, but once Dad has loaded up the luggage, the little car is looking pretty crowded. That's when Aunty Jill utters those fateful words, "Madonna, **you should** go in our car. We've got a lot more room."

In my mind, I scream "NO!" in reality, I nod with an, "Oh." Eight hours trapped in a car with Brains giving me quizzes, little Jack perfecting the art of being the annoying younger brother, and Mrs. Bossy giving me the entire 'you should' range from careers to hairstyles.

I'm about to climb into the car when Uncle Jim calls out, "Hang on, little mate," I freeze with my hand on the door handle. To my amazement, Uncle Jim pulls out one of those mini battery-powered vacuum cleaners and gives my shoes a quick vacuum over before he lets me in the car. He does everyone else's feet as well.

Brains looks at me with a sorry smile on her face and says, "You'll have to forgive Dad; he just loves his car."

We are heading to a place called Sandy River National Park, which I admit sounds nice but is unfortunately about eight hours drive away. Sometime after the first hour, my stomach starts to rumble and grumble. At first, it's not that loud, but the volume grows as time goes on. Soon both Brains and Jack obviously hear my stomach as they both start to give me some strange looks.

It gets worse; it was that big bag of prunes. I've gone past the stomach noises, now VERY, VERY smelly farts are escaping me.
Brains winds down her windows and sticks her head halfway out, while Jack just pinches his nose shut with his fingers and wiggles around on his seat.

Eventually, the smells reach Uncle Jim and Aunt Jill. I hear some groans and whispered conversation. Uncle Jim calls out, asking if anyone needs the toilet. How embarrassing! I try to build up my courage to admit I do when Jack beats me to it. He yells out, "Madonna needs to go, really bad!"

By the time Uncle Jim finds a toilet to stop at, I'm at a desperate stage. As soon as the car stops, I'm out the door, bolting for the toilet. I make it, but only just and have to spend more minutes sitting on the toilet than a civilized person ever should.

Finally, I'm able to return to the car; everyone is out walking around, stretching their legs, except for Uncle Jim, who is emptying a can of air freshener into the car interior. As we climb back into the car to continue the journey, the lemon smell is a bit over-powering but not as bad as the "*Madonna on prunes*" smell.

We eventually catch up with Mom and Dad when they stop for lunch at a little roadside seafood cafe. Mom and Dad order a big pile of prawns (we call them shrimp in America), and we all sit down at the table to eat. Now I've never eaten prawns before, but I am starving, so I grab one and shove it in my mouth and start chewing. It is TERRIBLE, all crunchy shell with sharp edges. It is so bad I grab a napkin and spit it out of my mouth.

As I take the napkin away from my mouth, I realize everyone is looking at me and laughing. "Madonna," Mom manages to gasp out between her bouts of laughter, "you have to peel the shell off the prawn before you eat them."

The second prawn tastes much better.

After lunch, it was only about three more hours before we reach Sandy River. Dad loves to stay in units when we go on holidays, while Mom loves to camp. One look at Sandy River National Park lets me know that this is definitely the camping section of our holiday. Sandy River has a river, a beach, lots of trees, some flat grassy areas, a brick fireplace, and an old wooden building. I assume that it must be the toilets and showers.

Mom's in her element and starts using phrases like "being one with nature" and "discovering the great outdoors."

Aunt Jill and Uncle Jim pull out three tents from their boot, so the parent couples have one tent each, and I and the dynamic duo share the other one. Of course, our tent has no instructions, so we have to figure out how to put it up by watching the adults. Dad was going to help us until Mrs. Bossy yelled out, "No, Bully, they need to learn to be self-sufficient!"

After a long hot hour, I learned two things: how to put up a tent and that having an IQ of 148 doesn't mean you know how to put up a tent. Luckily Jack and I were able to figure out where to put the poles and how to peg the tent down, while Brains just didn't get it.

Eventually, the tent was up. A bit lopsided and a bit wobbly, but we had somewhere to sleep. Jack and I get along surprisingly well, and Brains even thanks me for all my help. Maybe this holiday might be more fun than I thought.

With the tent up, my thoughts turn to the toilet again. NO PRUNES EVER FOR ME AGAIN!!!!!!! As I head off to the toilet, Jack calls out, "Don't look down!" with a laugh. A strange thing to say, I think to myself as I reach to open the toilet door. The sign reads…**Pit Toilet**.

When I open the door, the smell is terrible, but my need is so great that I HAVE to go in. Giant blowflies buzz around, the toilet seat looks normal (well, kind of normal – it is pink!), but I can't find any buttons to press to flush the toilet.

As I go to sit on the toilet seat…I look down into the toilet bowl. Now I understand! Now I know why Jack said don't look down. This toilet doesn't have a normal bowl; what you do in the toilet just drops into a big hole underneath, a giant pit! Guess that is why they call it a pit toilet. In the gloom of the pit, I can see and SMELL what has been done by whoever went before me.

Actually, I can see what was done by many people who went before me! GROSS!!!!! I hold my breath, finish my business and get out of there as fast as I can.

Back at the tent…Jack, Brains, and I do some bonding over how gross the toilet is. I'm feeling pretty tired and dirty, and I ask them where the showers are. They smile and point towards the beach. "Do you wash in the ocean?" I ask.

"No, Maddi, explains Jack, "there's a pipe sticking out of the dune with fresh water from an underground spring. The water constantly flows from the pipe."

"How do you shower in the open? People will see me," I say in a horrified voice.

"You wear your bikini; this is real camping," replies Jack.

I walk down to the beach with my bikinis on and my toiletry bag, hoping that the pipe shower is just a joke. No joke! There sticking out of the sandhill about 3 meters above me, is a rusty pipe. Flowing out of the pipe is a torrent of water. At least the water is clean and clear. I grab my shampoo and soap and jump under the water to discover it is FREEZING cold!

Mom would be proud. I set a new World Record for the fastest shower ever and then sprint back to our tent to change into my clothes.

That night we have dinner cooked on a BBQ, and afterward, we sit around the fire. Uncle Jim pulls out a guitar, and we sing along with him. Camping is fun. The night is clear, the stars are bright, and there is a huge full moon shining down on us.

We have the whole campground to ourselves. I think all the other campers have gone to the campgrounds that have real toilets and hot showers!

Eventually, Mrs. Bossy says we should all go to bed as she has a big day planned for tomorrow. I'm still a bit hungry, so I grab a loaf of bread out of the car and eat a few slices. I'm too tired to bother taking the bread back to the car, so I just leave it on the table with our plates and cutlery.

Sometime in the middle of the night, I wake up to a rustling sound. The full moon is shining brightly through our tent window, and I can see that both Brains and Jack are sound asleep. The rustling sound is coming from just outside our tent. Then I hear the plates being knocked off the table.

Someone is stealing our stuff! I creep across to the zippered door and start to unzip it slowly.

The rustling stops. I stop zipping. The rustling starts again. Very, very slowly, I start unzipping again until I can see outside.

Glowing in the moonlight are two yellow eyes. That's no person unless they are a zombie!!!!

As my eyes adjust to the light, I can see the eyes are attached to a small furry animal with a long curled tail. The eyes stop staring at me, and the creature returns to eating the bread on the table. I decide to go out for a closer look (I know this is incredibly brave!).

I'm sure it's a possum, and they are harmless, so I feel fairly safe. I walk right up to the end of the table…really close to it…and it still keeps eating, totally ignoring me.

Finally, it finishes the bread (no toast for breakfast), gives me one last look with those big eyes and jumps off the table, and wobbles into the nearby bushes.

I turn to go back to the tent.

I scream! I scream again!!

Eye to eye staring at me is a giant fur-covered creature. As I open my mouth for a third scream, the creature turns and hops away.

Uncle Jim appears at my shoulder, followed closely by my Dad.

"Don't worry mate, it's just a kangaroo," says Uncle Jim, "back to bed, everyone," he continues with a smile.

Wednesday

As the sun peeps over the horizon in the early dawn, Mrs. Bossy's whistle blasts me wide-awake. "Let's go, time to get up, everyone!" she yells, scaring all the little animals within a mile of the camp.

I scramble about in our tent in the gloom, trying to find my suitcase so I can change my clothes. After five minutes of searching through the mess in our tent, I realize that my suitcase must still be in the car (where the bread should be). I search both cars...no suitcase!

I tell Mom I think my suitcase got left behind at the unit in Sydney. "Don't worry, sweetie, after our walk, I'll call the unit managers and see if your suitcase is still there," says Mom, while Mrs. Bossy slowly shakes her head.

I am desperate to change my clothes! I wore the clothes I had on now all yesterday and last night, and they are starting to smell! But I smile and thank her.

Mrs. Bossy sets a cracking pace and booms at us to "keep up" as we have to be back by 7:30 am to have breakfast.

Breakfast is a bowl of cereal, so I don't know what the time deadline is all about. I suppose that is why I gave her the nickname of Mrs. Bossy.

We get back from the bushwalk. It is boiling here, and walking so quickly has made me sweat all over my clothes.

Mom phones the holiday unit manager while we are eating. She walks over smiling and gives me the good news...my suitcase was left on the front lawn of the units. Then comes the bad news… "and the lovely man is going to keep it safe for you until we return to Sydney."

Silence. I try to process what she has just said.

"Mom, I CAN'T wear the same clothes for the whole holiday!" I beg.

"It's okay Maddi, there is a shop at Brooms Head," Mrs. Bossy calls out.

I feel so relieved, "I'm so glad there are some fashion shops at Brooms Head."

"Not shops Maddi, there is only one shop. It sells everything from petrol, food, tools, books, and clothes," Mrs. Bossy replies with a smile.

Brains and Jack both have a little chuckle at that too. If I were a fan of those silly superhero movies, I'd say, "My spider senses are tingling," but obviously, I'm too cool for that.

Uncle Jim drives Mom and me into Brooms Head. It's a lovely place, nice beach, nice camping ground, nice petrol station, nice shop. Yes…that's right, shop, not shops. Mrs. Bossy is right; it does have everything, food, takeaways, postcards, fishing gear, surfing stuff, and even clothes.

There is a lovely collection of clothes that you can choose from; you can have bright orange tie-dye shirts and matching shorts or bright yellow tie-dye shirts and matching shorts. In my real life, I would never wear these clothes, but they are better than nothing.

Mom buys me the orange and yellow outfits. I change into the orange clothes in the change room (behind a shower curtain at the back of the shop).

When I come out, Mom gushes, "You look so gorgeous Madonna, I can remember wearing clothes like that when I was young." It is reassuring to know that my clothes were cool…in the 1980s!

When we arrive back at the campgrounds, my new outfit brings happiness to all. Everyone has a good laugh at me! I just smile.

We spend the rest of the day swimming and lazing around at the beach; it's a great day.

That night I wake up desperately needing to go to the toilet. Everyone else is fast asleep, and it is pitch black outside. I fumble around in the dark tent, trying to find a torch. I don't want to walk to the toilet in the dark on my own. I try to make a bit of noise so that Brains will wake up and come with me. People with big brains must go into a deep sleep because she doesn't even budge when I crawl across her feet.

Finally, I find the torch and *accidentally* shine it on Jack's face. Not surprisingly, he wakes up. After a bit of begging, Jack reluctantly agrees to accompany me to the toilets.

A thick cloud cover is blocking out the moon. It is so dark, apart from the narrow band of light coming from the torch. One torch, two people – didn't think that through! If I take the torch into the toilet, Jack will be outside in the dark all alone. There was NO WAY I was going into that pit toilet by myself in the dark.

I'm beginning to like Jack; he actually volunteered to stand outside in the dark while I took the torch into the toilet with me.

His last whispered instructions to me are to look after the torch; it is his Dad's super torch with a thousand different gadgets on it (I think that is a bit of an exaggeration). Jack told me it is only in our tent because he had borrowed it without asking.

The door creaks open, and all I can see is what's in the small circle of light from the torch. For such a **super torch**, it doesn't even give that much light. But there's enough light for me to see the spider webs hanging from the ceiling, some type of big black bug scuttling across the floor, and a giant moth that starts fluttering madly around the light from the torch. Creepy! It's like I have stumbled onto the set of a horror movie!

After checking the seat for spiders and with the smell reminding me NOT to look down, I sit down and start to do what I have to do. It's then I hear a noise, a dry scratching type of sound. A quick flash of the torch reveals that I am alone in the toilet, except for spiders, moths, and a bug. The noise keeps happening, so I rush to finish when I realize that the noise seems to be coming from the toilet itself. I'm finally ready to leave when I decide to break Jack's rule of *Don't Look Down* to see what makes that noise. As I shine the light down into the pit, I see a pair of slit-like eyes looking up at me. Just as my brain realizes what is looking up at me, a huge snake raises its head and hisses. At the same time, the giant moth in an effort to get to the torch light, crashes into my hand holding the torch. I scream and drop the torch into the pit.

My new favorite cousin, Jack, races into the toilet, shouting, "What's wrong!" I just point; it is as though I have lost the ability to speak. He comes in and stands beside me, and we peer into the pit. The torch is working, and its light is shining on the snake as it slowly moves towards the torch. The snake makes a sudden strike at the torch, grabbing it and swallowing it whole. The toilet is plunged into inky blackness. Both Jack and I scream, bolt from the room and run all the way back to the tent.

As we climb into our sleeping bags, Jack whispers, "Dad must never know we lost his torch."

Thursday

In the morning, I awake to the sound of a diesel engine rumbling away. The ranger runs a generator to power his tools as he does some maintenance on the toilet building.

My two cousins have already woken up and left the tent. I stumble outside in my yellow tie-dye outfit to see everyone standing around a table. I hear Uncle Jim saying, "I'm sure I left my torch right here on the table." Jack and I exchange worried and very guilty looks. I feel terrible and want to confess, but I promised Jack, and he is keeping a very close eye on me.

We have just finished breakfast when the ranger wanders over and says, "You folks might want to come and have a look at this." As we walk over to the area in front of the pit toilet, Jack gives me a worried look. "Now we are in deep trouble," he whispers.

The ranger stops and points to a giant snake lying dead on the ground. "I pulled it out of the pit toilet," he says. It was disgusting; it was covered in "you know what"! He hosed it off and pointed to a lump, "Look at this," he said. "I'm guessing it is something it swallowed and eventually choked on...probably a large bush rat or something," he explains. Jack and I look at each other.

The ranger tells us he will cut it open, as he is curious to see what the snake had caught. It is pretty gross when he starts to cut into the snake, I want to look away, but I can't. I have to know.

The ranger gasps with surprise when Uncle Jim's torch is revealed as the mystery lump. Surprisingly Uncle Jim seems quite happy, "Look, it is still working." He explains to the ranger how he had left his torch on the table; they agree that the snake must have taken it from there before crawling into the pit. The ranger hands back the torch to Uncle Jim, who gives it a quick wipe with a cloth.

I KNOW that Jack and I will NEVER touch that torch again, not ever!!!!!

We spend the morning kayaking in the little creek. It has beautiful, crystal clear water with little fish swimming around. The adults tried fishing, but secretly I was happy when they didn't catch anything. Those little fish are so cute and adorable.

My cousins and I are getting on well. We all paddle the kayak up the creek while our parents set up for a picnic lunch. Even Mrs. Bossy seems happy today, and she isn't bossing everyone around! Brains, Jack, and I sit in some shallow water telling funny stories when I decide to go for a swim to the middle of the creek. I lazily float on my back, watching the soft white clouds float past in the bright blue sky.

Suddenly my peaceful drifting is disturbed when I hear the sound of a large splash from the other side of the creek. I turn lazily to look and jerk upright rapidly. A large gray crocodile is swimming towards me! In a panicked flurry of arms, I explode into action and head towards the sandbank where Brains and Jack sit in the shallow water. I swim so fast that if I had been in the Olympics, I'm sure I would have won a gold medal! In between my frantic strokes, I try to scream a warning to my cousins.

Yes, that's me, Maddi, the hero. I can hear the news report now – "Maddi Bull is a true hero, despite being about to be torn *apart from a savage crocodile…this brave young girl unselfishly used some of her last breaths on Earth to warn her cousins."*

Unfortunately, my warnings sound more like panicked screams. It isn't until I reach the shallows and turn my swimming into running that I'm able to finally get out some clear, intelligible words, "Run, Run, Crocodile!

I am almost on the bank of the creek when I see my parents and Uncle and Aunty looking down into the water. How horrible, I think, for my parents to see their only daughter disappear into the jaws of a monster.

But then I hear laughter coming from the group of adults. Soon Brains and Jack join in the laughter too. Maybe they are just relieved that I am almost safe. I just keep running and throw myself into Dad's arms, still screaming.

Uncle Jim manages to stop his laughter long enough to gasp out, "That's not a crocodile; that's just a goanna." "Don't worry, Maddi. It won't hurt you. It is just a large lizard," he says, still smiling.

The goanna - formerly known as crocodile, looks at us, then it runs straight past. It now looks a lot smaller than it did in the water. It runs up a tree trunk and hides amongst the leaves. "Maddi," continues Uncle Jim, "we only have crocodiles in Northern Australia, thousands of miles away from here."

Dad took this photo of the goanna.
He says that one day I will laugh
about it. 😣

Friday

Today we leave Sandy River National Park and head to Yambucca Heads (who makes up these weird names!!!), moving on to civilization, as Dad calls it. It takes an hour to pack up the tents and another hour making sure not one tiny molecule of dirt or sand ends up in Uncle Jim's car. We have to vacuum everything before it goes into the car. Not even Mrs. Bossy can get him to hurry up.

Finally, we set off. This time I'm traveling with Mom and Dad!!! As I sit in the back in my matching tie-dye orange outfit, I ask the most important question.

"Are there any clothes shops in Yambucca Heads?" I ask.

Neither of my parents knows, so I'll just have to live in hope.

About two hours later, we arrive in Yambucca Heads. As we cruise up the one main street, one thing is clear. This is not civilization as we know it. Yambucca is a little fishing and surfing town with lots of fishing boats, a very old movie cinema which appears to only show old surfing movies, and three shops with surfboards for sale out the front.

The trendy, fully stocked fashion shop appears to exist only in my hopeful mind.

We find the campground we are staying at. It is at the end of the main (or should I say – only street).

For the first three days, we will be staying here, and then Dad gets his luxury, another three days in a house before we fly home.

We take the rest of the day setting up our tents. It is a lot different from Sandy River. Here there are heaps of tents crammed in together, and instead of the peaceful sounds of nature, all we can hear is the sounds of other campers.

The best news is that there are REAL toilets and hot showers!

Saturday

When Mrs. Bossy's whistle goes off in the morning, it doesn't worry me. I've been awake for ages. The sound of tent zips being opened and shut and lots of too loud voices from the little children (who seem to be overrunning this campground) woke me at sunrise.

After breakfast, Mrs. Bossy announces that we kids should spend the day at the campground's Kids' Club while the adults have some relaxation time.

Miss Jane is the lady in charge of the Kids' Club, and she is nice, but she talks to everyone like they are 4 years old. "Oh Maddi, what a lovely name," she gushes, "and darling, what cute little dimples you have."

How embarrassing!

Then she picks on Jack, "And you Jack, tell me darling, are you the little man of the family?" Jack's face went bright red.

Brains gives her a look that says: Don't Talk To Me!

The other children attending the Kids' Club are all playing in an undercover area. There are about 20 kids, and it is very clear that Brains and I are the oldest.

WELCOME TO YAMBUCCA KIDS CLUB

☺ Oh no! They are all young! ☹

The first hour passes at the speed of a wounded snail! Yes, we make macaroni necklaces! Miss Jane raves about Brain's necklace; she makes her stand up and show everyone. Brains looks like she wants aliens to abduct her.

There is something sweet about Miss Jane, though. She has a good heart and is trying her best to give us a good time. She calls everyone "darling," in fact; she uses darling in every sentence that comes from her sweet mouth. Her new name is going to be Miss Darling.

The second hour involves some chalk drawings on the concrete walkway and some face painting. Miss Darling lets Brains and I paint the little kids.

Brains paints her brother as the devil; he wants to be Superman, so he isn't happy when he looks in the mirror. Brains can't stop laughing, she has tears rolling down her face, and she starts snorting

We have a BBQ lunch. Over our burnt sausages, Brains and I shared our imaginings of how to escape Kids' Club.

Then Miss Darling announces that after lunch, we are playing volleyball.

Brains and I groan, apparently like me, Brains is no sporting legend. But when we see the volleyball court our faces light up. We strap on our kneepads and race to make sure we are on the same side.

Why so suddenly enthusiastic, you may ask? The net only comes up to our shoulders. After two games where we dominate, with great spikes and lots of high fives (we feel invincible, like superheroes), Miss Darling pulls us off the court to let the little kids have a fair game.

We end the Kids' Club session with a movie, I've already seen it, so I help Miss Darling clean up.

Brains has instant popularity status after the volleyball game and is sitting surrounded by little kids. They love her!

Finally, Mom collects us, and as we walk back to our tent site, I notice both Brains and Jack scratching their heads...a lot!

The next morning, Brain's hair looks like she has dreadlocks, and Jack's is even messier than usual. Both are still scratching at their heads madly. Then Mrs. Bossy utters those fearful words, "I think you've got head lice."

Uncle Jim says, "Don't worry, I can get rid of them into the tent, you two."

Mom and Dad commence a whispered conversation with Mrs. Bossy. Meanwhile, I hear a buzzing sound coming from the tent. When Jack and Brains emerge, I realize what Uncle Jim's headlice remedy is...he has shaved Jack's hair down to a stubble, and Brains hair isn't much longer.

Then Uncle Jim says, "Have you got them too Maddi, come over here, and I'll check your hair."

That's when Mom reminds me how much I love her, as she says, "No Jim, it's okay, I'll check Maddi's hair myself."

Fortunately, I have no headlice. Mom quietly reassures me that even if I did, she wouldn't allow Uncle Jim to shave my head.

Brains, Jack, and I go for a walk along the river. I tell Brains how sorry I feel for her. She is quite cool about it and tells me it is the third time she has had the same headlice treatment. "Don't worry, Maddi, it will grow back," she says, shrugging her shoulders.

As we walk past the playground near the beach, I notice some of the local kids staring at us. I'm wearing my tie-dye clothes today, and with Brain's shaven hair, we do stand out. Rudely they call out, "Hey baldy, what's with your friend's weird outfit!"

I whisper to Brains to just ignore them while little Jack slinks between us. As we continue to walk past, the insults keep flying.

Then I get one of my brilliant ideas. In my worst fake French accent, I say to the girl, "You do not understand. We have come directly from Paris. I point at Brains, "She is a famous French teen model, that is the hottest hairstyle in Paris right now, and this tie-dye print cost $100, and everyone over there is wearing them. I know your little town is a bit isolated, but I would have thought even here you'd have heard of the latest styles."

Before the locals even get a chance to reply, Brains bursts out with a torrent of French and extravagant gestures. We keep walking, leaving the local kids looking confused in our wake.

The three of us burst out laughing. Brains says, "That was so funny, Maddi!" I ask her how come she speaks French so well.

Her reply is typical, "I told you I'm a genius, Maddi. I speak French, Spanish, and Mandarin." We spend the rest of the day at the beach; holidays are so wonderful.

That night we head out for dinner at the local Chinese restaurant. It looks fancy and sits on top of the one hill in Yambucca Heads. The restaurant is crowded, but we get a table in about the middle of the restaurant. All the dishes have difficult to pronounce Chinese names. So, it's quite funny when Mrs. Bossy decides she will order for all of us.

In her loud voice, she struggles with the unusual words as she orders. From the look on the face of the waiter, he doesn't understand most of what she is trying to say. The first waiter calls a second waiter over when Mrs. Bossy tries to order a second time. She does just as bad a job at pronouncing the words…saying them slower and louder.

The two waiters are very polite, but you can see they are trying very hard not to laugh.

Just when it's looking like everyone at our table is going to die either of embarrassment or starvation, Brains saves the day. She bursts into some rapid-fire Chinese, quickly ordering our meals. I get the feeling she might have added a little joke about her Mom at the end, as both waiters had a little chuckle and a quick glance at Mrs. Bossy.

The meals are beautiful, and we all enjoy them. My favorite is a seafood dish with prawns, fish, and even whole tiny little octopuses. Brains is enjoying showing off her language skills and keeps having conversations with the waiters in Chinese as they bring out the different dishes.

One of the waiters is very young, only about our age. I'm guessing his family owns the restaurant. Brains seems to enjoy practicing her language skills on this boy. Every time he comes over to our table, he talks to Brains…but keeps glaring at me. I'm sure he's looking at me!

After a while, I have to say something to Brains, "That boy keeps staring at me," I whisper.

"I know," she replies, "I think he might like you."

My face goes instantly red but even redder when Brains tells me she will ask him why he is looking at me!

"No!" I whisper-shout (didn't you know you could shout and whisper at the same time, you learn something every day).

Brains ignores me and bursts into Chinese, and the boy answers…looking at me again.

When he has left, I ask what he said. Brains answers, "He said you have beautiful eyes."

My face goes into full meltdown mode; I almost slide under the table.

As everyone has finished their meals, we are walking out to the front of the restaurant while Dad and Mrs. Bossy pay the bill.

Suddenly I hear a voice calling, "Miss, miss, please wait." I turn to see the young waiter hurrying towards me. He stops in front of me and smiles. Then he reaches a hand out towards my face. My brain is racing; what is he doing?

His fingers gently pull a tiny little octopus (from my seafood meal) out of my hair.

"Your friend told me you were keeping this for a late-night snack, but I think she was just playing a trick on you," he explained.

I mumble an embarrassed thanks and rush after Brains. She was nearly crying; she is laughing so much.

"Now that I think about it," she says, "Maybe it was the octopus' eyes that he thought were beautiful."

Monday

I wake up the following day in a very happy mood; last night was our last night in the tent. Today we move into Dad's style accommodation, an actual house that Dad has rented for us. It's called the 'Blue House,' it turns out it's just down the road from the camping ground. When we first see it, we feel pretty disappointed; it's a dump.

Dad looks pretty dejected too, as he booked it, but when we go inside all our faces light up. It's fantastic! It's cool. It's been completely renovated and is very modern and perfectly clean.

The best part is that the kids have a separate area with a TV, bunk beds and a heap of board games. The board games didn't feel as exciting though after Brains beat me at scrabble three times in a row by about one hundred points using words that I couldn't even spell. I didn't even know what they meant, but sure enough, every one of them was in the dictionary.

When we explore the house, we discover an unusual design feature; the downstairs definitely hasn't been renovated. An old creaky, dark stairway leads down to the underneath; we are talking creepy, serious horror movie creeps.

So Creepy!!!!! 😲

The floor was plain concrete, the walls were also rough concrete, and the ceiling was just open rafters. The lights were just bare bulbs.

In the middle of this dusty dim dungeon-like room sat a shiny white bath on claw feet with rusty taps coming up from the floor. I stare at the bath and think, 'No way am I sitting down here in that.'

"How cool! I can't wait to have a bath down here!" Brains announces.

Jack holds my hand and shakes his head.

So is born my idea of revenge on Brains for the waiter joke.

That night, Brains collects her toiletries and heads downstairs to enjoy her bath. I try to enlist Jack's help, but when I combine downstairs and dark in one sentence, he runs and hides under his blanket on his bed.

Ah well, it looks like this will be a solo mission for Maddi the brave. Fortunately for me, the light switch for the whole downstairs area is at the bottom of the stairway, and the stairway is enclosed, so Brains can't see me from the bath. I slowly make my way down the stairs, wincing at each creak as my feet go from one step to the next.

I needn't worry about Brains hearing me as she is singing. The term singing covers a wide range of sounds. Let's just say, American Idol contestants...you have nothing to fear from Brains!

I'm just reaching toward the light switch when I hear the door at the top of the stairway swing and close with a bang. It cuts out the light from upstairs, and now the stairway is quite dark, and I can just see the light switch.

The bang of the door cuts through Brains singing. She stops, obviously listening, wondering what the noise is. Perfect, I can feel her tension building. "Who's there?" she calls out in a nervous voice.

That's when I strike…reaching out and hit the light switch, plunging the entire room and stairway into complete darkness.

Brains screams. I scream louder and, in panic, can't find the light switch. As I am fumbling around trying to find the lights, Brains comes flying around the corner and smashes into me. We both scream again in unison as we fall in a heap on the floor.

Suddenly the stairway is flooded in light as Mrs. Bossy appears at the top of the stairs. "What on Earth are you girls doing?" she booms.

In the light, our fear evaporates, and we both start laughing as Brains realizes what I was up to. We are still chuckling over dinner, although I'm not sure Mrs. Bossy finds it as funny as we do.

Tuesday

Brains, Jack, and I are walking down to the beach when we hear someone yelling. We turn around to see the girl who was harassing us the other day rushing towards us. "Oh no," I groan.

While Jack whispers, "Let's just run!"

"No," Brains says, "check her out."

"Bonjour!" the girl calls out with a big smile on her face.

I have to bite down hard on my tongue to stop laughing. She has cut her hair very short and is wearing a tie-dye top (obviously homemade). She even put tie-dye material on her boots.

I break out my terrible French accent again and say, "Oh wonderful! You are the height of fashion now! I bet everyone in town is looking at you!"

Brains starts speaking French again, with a couple of sentences that make no sense to anyone else. As we go our separate ways, everyone has a smile on their face.

Once we are far enough away so she can't hear us, Brains says, "Maddi, let that be a lesson to you, never be a slave to fashion." I glance down at my own tie-dye outfit and think no one can ever accuse me of being fashionable.

That night, I looked everywhere, trying to find my book, but it's nowhere to be seen. I'm about to give up when Jack whispers to me, "I think Jenny hid it downstairs." I thank Jack for the tip-off and head down the stairway to collect my book. I get to the bottom and discover my book sitting on the edge of the bathtub. That should have been enough warning for me. I hear the door at the top of the stairs bang shut and the sound of the bolt sliding across to lock it. I feel a shiver run up my spine at the thought of being locked up in this scary room.

But then I remember two other doors down here, one that goes out into the backyard through a little laundry. I rush over to the one leading to the side yard and am about to open it when I hear voices outside. Yes, of course, Brains and Jack have realized I'll try to escape through the closest door. They'll be waiting there to scare me when I come out. Except I'm way too smart for them, I creep away from the side door and head towards the door that leads to the backyard. I'll go out the back door, sneak around to the side door where they're waiting for me and scare them first.

The locking bolt on the side door is very rusty, and even though I try very hard, it still makes quite a loud noise as I work it loose. I stay still for a moment, hoping that no one hears me unlocking the door. The only thing I can hear is my own heartbeat and breathing. I smile in anticipation of scaring my cousins as I swing open the door. Suddenly I jump back in fright as a pair of hands appear in front of my face and clap twice loudly. I scream and fall back through the door landing on my bottom.

Brains steps through the door laughing hysterically, "Got you," she gasps between laughs. We walk up the stairs arm in arm…like the best friends we have become. Jack scrambles up behind us, his big smile reflecting his joy in helping to trick me.

Thursday

Our final day, we all feel pretty sad as we pack up and leave the little blue house and Yambucca heads.

I have fun with my cousins on the trip back to Sydney but knowing that soon we will have to say goodbye puts a damper on the trip.

Before you know it, we are at the airport, after a detour to pick up my suitcase that was left at the units. A quick change in the airport toilets sees me back in normal clothes at last.

We say our sad farewells to our relatives, with promises from them to visit us next year.

Boarding the plane, I look out for Miss Perfect, but she is nowhere to be seen. The trip home seems quicker, probably because I sleep most of the way. I didn't even notice Dad's snoring or Mom's singing.

Monday Morning

My first day back at school today, I've missed two weeks and dread to think of how much work I have to catch up.

A bigger shock is when I walk into class and discover a new girl sitting next to my very good friend, Richard…also known as Mr. Tall Dark and Handsome.

I sit next to my other friend Gretel. After a welcome hug and a few "I missed you so much," …I get straight to the point. "WHO IS THAT next to Mr. TDH?"

Gretel asks me, "Do you mean the tall slim beautiful girl with the long blonde hair?"

"Of course, I mean her," I replied gruffly.

Gretel tells me she is a new girl at our school, Linda Douglas; she continues on by also telling me that she isn't very nice.

"Why is she sitting next to Mr. TDH then?" I ask.

"Probably because she looks nice," replies Gretel with a weak smile.

At lunch, I get to meet Linda. When I say hi to Mr. TDH, he seems happy to see me, and I start to entertain him with my highly amusing stories from my holiday to Australia.

Then along comes Linda and interrupts us. "You must be the girl who was on holiday in Australia. Michelle, isn't it?"

"No, my name is **Maddi**."

Linda continues with, "Whatever, look at that hair. Did you leave your brush back in Australia?" She smiles and pulls her sleek blonde hair away from her face. "Anyway, Maddi, run along now. I need to speak to Richard about an assignment we are going to do together," says Linda as she drags Mr. TDH away by the arm.

After lunch, I sit next to Gretel, still fuming over Linda's treatment of me. "Don't worry about her, Maddi; you should have seen her last week with our buddy class. Her little buddy messed up her perfect hair, and Linda yelled at him and made the poor kid cry."

I can't help but watch her, she's mean, and she's sitting next to Mr. TDH.

That's when I notice that she seems to be scratching her head a lot, so much that her perfect hair isn't looking so perfect anymore.

Suddenly it clicks. I ask Gretel who Linda's buddy was?

"Harry," she replies with a smirk on her face. Harry is also known as *Harry Headlice*. Harry is one of those unfortunate children who always seem to have a case of head lice.

A great plan hatches in my brain while the rest of the class does math.

This is my plan:

Contact Brains and ask her to write two letters to Linda's parents – a headlice notice from my school and a second letter explaining the latest chemical-free way to beat headlice - all the way from Australia.

Follow Linda home, so I know where she lives.

Put Brain's letters in her letterbox - addressed to her parents.

Okay, I felt like a stalker following her home, but a girl's got to do what a girl's got to do!

I phone Brains, and she is excited to hear from me. "Oh Maddi, you are so naughty! Of course, I will help you; give me an hour."

With that, she got straight to work. The email arrives in under an hour.

I dress in dark clothes, put on a big floppy hat, casually walk to Linda's house, and put the letters in their letterbox.

Tuesday

The next day, the success of my plan is plain to see. Linda's long blonde hair is gone…replaced by very short hair. I guess that means no more mean comments about other girls' hair.

That night I email Brains thanking her for the two letters. It's great having a super smart cousin.

Now I have to figure out how to get Linda moved from sitting next to Mr. TDH.

BOOK 4

MY NEW BUDDY

Friday

My eyes creep to the clock for the 20th time, still not lunchtime! Mrs. Snow White, our history teacher, obviously not her real name, unless I'm enrolled at Disney School, drones on and on and on...

I have a liking for giving the people in my life nicknames, and I think it makes my life a bit more interesting. Her real name is Mrs. Tompkins, but Snow White suits her so much more. Her hair is midnight black in color and straighter than my ruler. It falls in an unmoving mass down her back with a fake flower pinned to her head in case one crazy strand tries to get out of place. Her skin is white...not that I don't go out much white...but more like Casper the Ghost white! Above her super intense blue eyes hang two very severe super thin eyebrows that add a slightly surprised but sinister expression to her face.

Mrs. Snow White is not the class's favorite teacher, and unlike the pleasant Fairy Tale character, she is strict and very harsh with us. I know what you're thinking...yes, she does sound a bit more like the evil queen but trust me on appearance, she's way too pretty to be an evil queen.

My twenty-first glance at the clock reveals two minutes to go!

Mrs. Snow White seems to have that ability that only certain special teachers have. The ability to make time stand still.

Suddenly my ears are alerted to a strange sound, the sound of silence. I can't hear any sounds in our classroom at all. Not Mrs. Snow White's voice, not the whispering of the two boys behind me, not even the scratching of Gretel's pencil (my best friend who is sitting next to me as she frantically takes notes as always). Not even the ticking of the wall clock I spent so much time staring at.

I glance around the room, no noise, no talking, no movement, nothing! Mrs. Snow White has finally done it. She has actually made time stop altogether. Everyone, everything, is frozen in time! Except for me, it must be my incredible skill to NOT listen that has let me escape the amazing powers of Mrs. Snow White.

I stand up and start to cautiously move around the room, staring at my frozen classmates. I stop in front of Mr. Tall Dark and Handsome, real name Richard. I wave my hands in front of his face - no reaction, not even a blink.

Just as well, it probably would have been so embarrassing if he wasn't really frozen still.

Time to have some fun. Sitting next to Mr. TDH is Linda Douglas. Linda seems determined to come between me and Mr. Tall Dark and Handsome, and has ruthlessly pursued him. I grabbed Linda's hand and brought it up towards her face. I straightened out one of her fingers and pushed it up her nose as far as it will go. I step back to admire my handy work with a laugh when an idea springs to mind.

I race back to my desk, peeled off a pea-sized piece of dried glue from my glue bottle, and use a pen to color it green.

I rush back to Linda and remove the finger from her nose, and carefully placed the green-colored glue on the tip of her nostril. The glue stuck nicely. This should be a good look when time starts up again.

Next, I move to Peter Kirk, the meanest bully in the class. On the way, I gently remove the lovely pink bow Melody likes to wear in her hair and carefully transfer it into Ted's unruly spikey hair

Finally, I moved to Mrs. Snow White, who was sitting at the teacher's desk at the front of the room. I stand back and consider my options.

I spot a very thick marker pen on her desk. I quickly grab the pen and remove the lid. I use my best art skills to swiftly do one very thick red eyebrow over Mrs. Snow White's severe thin one.

I stepped back and admired an eyebrow that any clown would be proud of.

My work is done, and in fear that time may restart at any moment, I hurriedly return to my desk. I sit and stare at the clock, smiling at the thought of what will happen when my tricks are revealed.

Gradually I grow tired and feel my head drift towards the desk. I'm aware of the thump of my head on the desk, fractionally ahead of hearing the sound of the lunch bell.

As I lift my dazed head, I realize two things. I must have fallen asleep, and that I can hear many of my classmates laughing. I open my eyes with the expectation of seeing the laughing children staring at Linda, Peter, and Mrs. Snow White.

In horror, I realize they are staring and laughing at me!

Mrs. Snow White, with her thin eyebrows raised, asks if I have finished my little rest. Linda is standing next to Mr. TDH with no pretend snot on her nose and Peter with no pink ribbon in his hair. Oh no, it was all a dream!

Most of the lunchtime involves dealing with my classmates and their funny comments about me falling asleep in class. This may take a long time to live down.

The rest of the day passes quickly, and I happily escape school to rush home.

Home! My mom, whom I call Mrs. Absolutely Positive, greets me as I enter the lounge room. "I bet you had a marvelous day at school, another fulfilling step on your life of learning," she gushes. Now you know where her nickname came from! She means well, but her constant positiveness sometimes collides with my reality of being an almost cool girl.

Dad, Mr. Boom Boom, is on his way home. Mom says when he gets home, we're all going to pick up a surprise dad has organized. Dad's previous surprises have included me joining a soccer team and doing a two-day circus trapeze course. You can understand why I feel a little nervous.

Dad arrives home, and soon all three of us are back on the road heading off somewhere. Mom and dad were all smiles and happiness, and from the conversations, it seems that I'm the only one in the dark about the surprise.

We finally arrive at the front gate of what appears to be a small farm.

Dad jumps out and opens the gate, and Mom drives through with Dad reclosing the gate after us.

We then bump down a little dirt track until we reach a small farmhouse.

Dad ushers us up to the front door, where we are met by a really old lady.

I heard those magic words every child loves to hear, "You must be the puppy's new family?"

I pretty much didn't hear anything else after that.

The lady let us out to her backyard with the cutest little puppy I had ever seen stood wagging a tiny little tail. It waddled over to me, and when I reached down towards it, the puppy rolled over onto its back and presented his tummy to me for a tummy rub.

"It looks like Buddy, and you will be great friends," said the lady. "Boston Terriers have such lovely natures."

I gaze up at my parents with the puppy now sitting at my feet. "Is he really ours?" I asked.

Both my parents smile, and Dad replies in what is a whisper to him so as not to scare the puppy, "Yes, Maddi, we thought a new puppy would be good for all of us, especially our Great Dane Tyson."

During the trip home, Buddy is so super-duper cute. He curls up and buries his head under my arm. Every now and again, he raises his head and licks my hand wagging his cute little tail. I whisper into his little ear that we will be friends forever, and I will always look after him.

Friday Night

Mom let Buddy sleep in my room as it's his first night with us. After tonight his bedroom would be the laundry as he needs to have his own place to sleep, and it has a tiled floor. I didn't argue; I was just happy to have Buddy in my room for tonight.

I am way too excited to sleep...at first, preferring to play with Buddy. Unfortunately, he keeps falling asleep, but I stay awake for hours just staring at him.

Eventually, I fell asleep on the floor next to him. The newspapers mom made me spread on the floor are a bit annoying; they rustled every time I move. I wake to a cold, wet nose pressed into my face with a loud sniffing noise.

So tired! I crawl back onto my bed and try to go to sleep. But I was now wide-awake! He keeps running around making his playing with his squeaky toy and jumping up onto the side of the bed, trying to pull himself up to me. I give in, even though I know he's not supposed to be on the bed, and pull him up.

No sleep for Maddi. After about an hour...the Buddy battery goes flat, and he falls asleep lying on my feet. At last, a chance to sleep, but I couldn't fall back to sleep with him on my feet. So very, very slowly, I edge one foot out from underneath him. Buddy stirs but doesn't wake up. Now for the second foot, slowly and carefully as his head is balanced on it. I almost have it out when those beautiful puppy eyes snap open, the tail starts wagging, and I endure another 20 minutes of play.

Finally, Buddy is totally exhausted and collapses on my face. This isn't going to work! I gently pick him up and put him on his soft and fluffy bed on the floor. Ahhh...sleep time.

I fall into a deep sleep, only to wake up a short time later, as Buddy licks my hand that is hanging over the side of my bed. Playtime starts again until finally, I fall into such a deep sleep. I am no longer aware if Buddy was awake or asleep.

When next I finally open my eyes, it is daylight. I stay as still as a store dummy, hoping that Buddy is still asleep and I could drift back to sleep. Then my nose detects a rather unpleasant odor, definitely a poo smell. Buddy was still sleeping on his bed but had left three lots of tiny puppy poos around the room. Good news, bad news. Two of the piles of poo were on the newspaper, yay! One missed the newspaper and is on the wooden floor, not so yay!

I creep out of my room to tell Mom of the poo emergency. She is very unsympathetic. She said, "Well, Madonna (as soon as she called me Madonna, I knew this was going to end badly), part of being a responsible pet owner is not just playing with your dog but feeding and cleaning up after him. You know where the cleaning stuff is, so best you get busy."

The bits on the paper are easy. I just rolled up the paper, poo and all, drop them into a bag, and then tie up the ends. It wasn't too hard to hold my breath that long.

The one on the wooden floorboards is not so easy and quick. Gingerly I got a bag and tried to scoop it up in one go. I think I deserve a C minus for poo scooping. I get some poo on the top of the bag. Have you ever tried to tie up a plastic bag with poo on the top ends? Believe me, it's not easy, and I got poo all over my fingers.

Brainwave! I grab a second bag and drop the first bag inside it and quickly tie it. However, a large amount of poo stays on the floor; in fact, it is now smeared all over the floor. YUCK! I ran off to get paper towels from the kitchen to wipe them up.

Disaster! Buddy has woken up, just what I needed! And he is running around the room with one of his toys. Sounds cute, but only if you didn't notice that he had run through the poo still on the floor and spread it around many other places.

Then one of those -please freeze the time moments- came along. Buddy was looking at my bed, his ears were pointing backward, and I could read his mind. He was going to jump on my bed! He had poo on his paws. A disaster was about to happen...and then he jumped. My cream-colored fluffy blanket was covered with brown icky sticky poo! I felt like vomiting! It was disgusting!

The cleaning job is spiraling out of control.

I take buddy outside and hose him off and dry his feet. Leaving Buddy or Mr. Mess (as I'm thinking of changing his name to) outside. I snuck my blanket outside and hosed it off, too, then I tiptoe to the laundry and put it in the washing machine.
Finally, I head back to my room and scrub off any remaining poo and mop the entire floor. Lucky for Buddy that I love him!

Monday

I didn't want to go to school today; I'd much rather have stayed home and played with Buddy. This is the second week with our new principal, Mrs. Cook.

Our old principal Mr. Hi-5 had decided to retire. As you can tell from his name Mr. Hi-5 was a pretty nice principal, he knew all the kids by name and used to walk around high-fiving kids at lunchtime.

I don't think he did anything else, but at least he was pleasant to the kids.

Mrs. Cook has only appeared in public once in the two weeks since she has taken over as the school principal. She came to assembly once and briefly went mad at the whole school because there was some litter on the edge of the oval.

She is a medium height, an older lady (probably about 100...okay, maybe 70) with very short iron-gray hair and a pair of glasses with a colorful frame that the English singer, Elton John, would have been proud of.

Obviously, a nickname for her was no challenge. Granny sprang to mind immediately. But not like a kindly granny in the TV shows...more like the sinister mean granny in those scary movies.

The second time she was spotted outside her office was when she once again suddenly showed up on parade.

Our deputy principal, Mrs. She Who Runs the School, was actually in the middle of handing out Student Awards. I thought- *that's nice Mrs. Cook must want to meet the students who won the Student of the Week Awards in person,* wrong!

As my class is at the front of the assembly, we heard the whispered conversation between Mrs. Cook and her deputy principal. Mrs. Cook first snatched the microphone out of the deputy's hand then quietly but harshly said, "You are letting the assembly make way too much noise! I can't work in my office with all this noise."

Mrs. She Who Runs the school looks confused, then annoyed. She replies just as curtly, "Mrs. Cook, they are just clapping the students of the week as they receive their certificates."

Mrs. Cook put a little more ice in her voice and instructed the Deputy to give out the rest of the certificates quickly and instruct the children to hold the applause and let them give one short clap at the end for all the certificate winners.

With that, she dropped the microphone onto the ground, which sent a sonic boom through the speakers...then she stormed off with the clicking of her high heels.

The Deputy Principal let out a sigh, bent down, and picked up the microphone. Following Mrs. Cook's instructions, she quickly finished the parade.

So, Gretel and I walked around the corner heading towards our PE lesson in the hall after changing into our sports clothes. We bumped into Mrs. Cook, who was rushing around the corner in the opposite direction. Gretel and I came out with sorry at the same time as Mrs. Cook snapped, "Why aren't you girls in class?" Before we can even reply, she continues, "Those aren't your correct uniforms! Report to the office for detention at lunchtime." She's strutted off with her high heels clicking without a backward glance.

Gretel and I hurry off to the PE lesson, upset for getting in trouble. We explain to Mr. Grant why we were late and how we got in trouble just for being in our gym gear. He gets that *look* on his face that all teachers get when they don't agree with something another teacher did or said...but don't want to say anything.

You know the same look that your mom or dad gets when they don't agree with what the other one has said you can or can't do.

Mr. Grant shook his head and said, "Don't worry, girls, I'll talk to Mrs. Cook and sort this out."

Mr. Grant hopped on the phone, and after about a 10-minute conversation that featured about 50 *buts* from him, he hung up. He sighed then, with a smile, said, "Your detention is canceled, girls."

We were very relieved and very grateful to Mr. Grant...he is such a cool teacher!

Thankfully the rest of the day passed smoothly, and I rush home to spend some time with Buddy. I burst through the front door and call out his name...but Mom shushes me and points to Buddy's bed. The sweet little thing is curled up and sound asleep.

Later that night, I regret letting him stay asleep. When Mom arranged the laundry for Buddy to sleep in, I didn't argue, no way I could survive another sleepless night like last night.

Did I mention my bedroom is quite close to the laundry? Yes, very close! In fact, close enough that I could hear Buddy scratching at the laundry door clearly. So close that when Buddy's scratching on the doorway didn't work, I could hear the whimpering and howling so clearly that he could have been in the same room. I tried ignoring it, I tried my fingers in my ears, I tried holding my pillow over my head, but nothing worked. Three times I went to the laundry and patted him until he fell asleep. Each time I had to be a ninja and creep soundlessly from the room.

Eventually, I fell into such a deep sleep that I wouldn't have heard a jet taking off in the house, let alone Buddy's demands for company.

I still felt tired, but not as bad as the previous morning when I woke up.

I tip-toed out to the laundry, which was strangely quiet.

Slowly I opened the door and peered inside. All occupants of the laundry were fast asleep, yes that's right, I said all occupants.

Little Buddy slept peacefully in his comfortable bed while Mom and Dad slept leaning against each other sprawled on the hard tile floor.

Obviously, now was not a good time to say good morning, so I quietly snuck back out, had my breakfast, and headed off to school.

Wednesday

Mrs. Cook ruined my day today, something I feel she may make a habit of doing. Today she announced in the school newsletter that it was compulsory for all students to compete in the school swimming carnival on Friday.

For the carnival, the school is divided into different sports houses, and all the kids compete against each other, scoring points in all the events to decide the Champion sports house. I'm in the blue house, called sharks.

Normally, that would be no major problem. I would make sure that mom didn't get the newsletter and develop a terrible mystery illness that, unfortunately, would keep me home from school on Friday.

However, her second announcement destroyed that plan quickly; she was pleased that from now on, a copy of the newsletter would now be emailed directly to all parents to ensure no parent missed out on vital school information. In other words, in case some students made sure that the paper newsletter never made it home!

I can swim...but I'm no Olympic swimmer, and the idea of floundering around in the pool while Mr. TDH looks on is not my idea of fun.

A brilliant idea strikes me! Perhaps I can get into mom's email account and delete the newsletter. All hope is not lost yet. On arrival at home, I immediately sense that my plan is doomed. Lying on the table is a pack of bright blue-colored paper, some cardboard toilet rolls, masking tape, blue body paint, and scariest of all - a can of blue hair coloring spray.

Mom had seen the email version of the school newsletter already. Drats!

My mom is great, please don't think me ungrateful, but she can get a little bit carried away sometimes. Yes, when Mrs. Absolutely Positive gets an idea, she can get way too excited...verified by her next statement, "So Maddi, I read about the swimming carnival, and I've grabbed a few items. You may not be the best swimmer, but when I finish with you, you'll certainly look like the best supporter."

The afternoon is spent making pom-poms and mom experimenting with her artwork on my face, arms, and legs. She was super keen to cover me in blue body paint, but I drew the line with that and the spray on blue hair colorant as I had memories of how hard it was to wash out from another time when Mom dressed me up as a frog for a dress-up-day at school.

As a good daughter, I let Mom have her fun; I even use the pom-poms as I did my house war cry. Mom loves it, but there's no way I'll ever be doing that in public.

My voice is so out of tune, and my dance moves with the pom poms are just plain dangerous. I look and sound so bad that Buddy runs off to the laundry and hides in his bed with his paws covering his ears.

Luckily, after a hot bath and a bit of vigorous scrubbing, I'm transformed from a 'mom's gone mad with the blue drawings on my arms and face girl' back into ordinary old Maddi.

Friday

Mom wakes me at 6, an hour earlier than usual, to get me made up for the swimming carnival. By the time Mom has finished with me, I am blue from my hair to the Blue Socks on my feet. This is much worse than when we had a practice; Mom has gone totally over the top!

Dad comes in and announces how amazing I look; I just think I look like an extra from that Avatar movie.

My hair is thickly coated with blue spray and pulled back into a ponytail. If it feels thick and stiff and just yuck, my skin which is covered with blue body paint (I couldn't stop her), feels itchy and irritated.

It is going to be a long, long day.

Mom is so proud of her handiwork; she insists on taking me to school. Proudly she walks with me to my classroom. I don't see anyone else with colored skin or colored hair. Most people have a house-colored shirt on, the girls have a matching ribbon in their hair, and some of the kids have a colored armband. I start to get a very bad feeling!

Mom whispers to me, "So many of your classmates have no team spirit."

A moment later, we arrive at my classroom door. Granny (Mrs. Cook) stands outside my classroom; her piercing steel-colored eyes look me up and down. She frowns and turns towards mom, "Are you responsible for the way this child is dressed?" she asks in a, *not at all friendly* tone.

Oblivious to Granny's obvious displeasure, mom starts to gush on about how she certainly was responsible for my appearance. "It wasn't easy," she said, and then she continued on about how she doesn't mind as she feels that it is essential for parents to show their support for school events.

Granny simply said, "Come to my office now!" Mom looked at me with a puzzled expression as we followed Granny to her office.

Once there, Granny quickly asks me for my name and then starts addressing mom as Mrs. Bull. Mom puts out her hand and introduces herself, "So pleased to meet you. My name is Mary..." Granny cuts her off.

"Mrs. Bull," replies Granny.

"Yes, that's me, and my first name is Mary." Mom continues, "And what is your first name?"

"Mrs. Cook," Granny replies yet again.

"No first name?" asks mom, in a not-so-friendly tone of voice.

"Not at school," replies Granny. "I believe that using first names of my staff implies a lack of respect."

Mom just lets out an "Oh..." in response to this.

Granny sits at her desk without inviting mom or me to sit. "Mrs. Bull, I have gone to great lengths to ensure that all parents are aware of my new school policy on sports competitions at school. I sent out a newsletter in both electronic and hard copy," she explains in a sarcastic tone.

"Of course, Mrs. Cook, I saw the email version; that's how I knew which day to prepare Maddi for the carnival."

Granny turned her computer screen around towards Mom and asked her to read the third paragraph under the swimming carnival out loud.

Mom complies, in a voice that gets softer as she reads on, "Students may wear a house colored shirt and girls a ribbon in their hair and boys an armband. No student is to have colored body paint or hair color. Pom-poms are also banned as they make a mess."

"Oh! I'm sorry," Mom apologizes. "I must have missed that bit when I read about the carnival. Although I must admit that it seems a pity for the children to miss out on the full dress-up experience."

"Well, that's the new rule, so I'm afraid your daughter will have to return home and remove all that blue from her hair and body," replied granny.

Mom then asks, "So which parent committee meeting did you get this rule approved at Mrs. Cook because I go to all of them, and to be honest, I can't remember that rule ever being discussed and approved?"

Granny stutters and stammers and finally blurts out, "I haven't actually had it approved by the parent committee yet, but I'm confident it will be."

Mom smiles, "In that case, Madonna, you had better head back to your class and get ready for the swimming carnival because, as Mrs. Cook knows...any rule changes have to be approved by the parent committee before they become official rules. Isn't that right, dear?" she asks Mrs. Cook.

Granny's mouth looks like she has just eaten a whole lemon, reluctantly she replies, "Yes, that's right, you may go to the carnival."

Mom's positive power wins over grumpy power.

My happiness continues as I join the class heading off to the swimming pool. My cool status is running high, as I am the only one with colored body paint and hairspray. Gretel and Mr. Tall Dark and Handsome are super impressed. At that moment, forget...*almost cool*, I'm totally cool! Okay, some of the cool gloss disappears when I get carried away and try some cheerleading moves with my pom-poms. And it slides even lower when I sing some of our team songs. But being the only fully blue colored team member still outweighs that.

***

However, as my turn to race draws closer...my nerves begin to grow. I'm not the best swimmer, and I didn't want to embarrass myself in front of Mr. TDH.

Then Gretel gave me some great advice; I should try and get a fantastic start, then at least I could say I lead the race for a little while.

Suddenly, my race is called to the starting blocks. And as I stand on the blocks, the end wall looks a long, long way away.

More pressure, Linda Douglas is lined up next to me. My brain thunders - must beat Linda, must beat Linda...hush brain, I'm trying to concentrate on the start.

From the corner of my eye, I see the starter raise his arm with the starting pistol. My leg muscles tense and suddenly spring off the blocks. I soared through the air, my body in a perfect dive position.

What a start, what reflexes! Just before my arms glide into the water, I hear the starter pistol, then a second crack from the starting pistol.

Oh no! False start! My head surfaces above the water, and I turned in my lane to swim back to the wall. Half the swimmers are still on the blocks, while half are in the pool with me swimming back to the wall. They must have followed me in when I false-started.

As I swim back to the wall, I notice the water in my lane is blue, I look over my shoulder, and a stream of blue is following me. The area surrounding the pool is quiet, with no race to cheer. Everyone is sitting and watching, wondering what will happen next.

In the quiet, Linda's voice, who didn't false start with me, is incredibly loud and clear. "Look! Maddi peed in the pool. The water around her is turning blue!"

This creates a frenzy of girls kicking and splashing to escape the spreading blue-colored water. I try to protest my innocence, but I'm not heard above the noise of squealing swimmers and laughing spectators.

The teachers send us all back to our team areas. Gretel and Mr. TDH try to shelter me from the teasing, and I remove my swimming goggles, revealing blue circles around my eyes. Most of the blue hair spray has washed out of my hair.

All the teachers are meeting on the pool deck, and I could see Granny throwing her arms around in an angry manner.

Mr. Grant, the PE teacher, comes over to me and looks at my blue circled eyes, and asked was that colored hairspray in my hair. After I tell him that it was blue, he smiles and replies, "That's a relief."

He walks over to the other teachers and Granny. After a few minutes of discussion, Granny grabs the microphone and announces, "The pool will not have to be drained, and the carnival will continue. Maddi Bull did not urinate in the pool; I repeat Maddi Bull did not urinate in the pool; the carnival will continue."

The race is rerun, but happily, for me, I'm disqualified for starting before the starter's gun went off. At least I don't have to worry about turning the water blue again. I try to blend in with the rest of the spectators, which isn't really that easy when your skin is still bluish. Most of the blue paint that was protected by my goggles wipes off onto my towel.

Finally, the day ends, and I rush home. Mom greets me enthusiastically as always. I skip the bit about being disqualified and suspected of urinating in the pool. I just tell her it was an exciting day. Then I rushed off to the bathroom to start the transformation from an oversized Smurf back to myself.

Sunday

After the usual three hours of Sunday morning housework, the house looks spotless. For an alternate hippie-style mother, mom can be very conventional when it comes to clean and tidy...especially my bedroom. I realize that despite how much I love little Buddy, he can be quite painful with the way he chews up everything in reach of his mouth. Who could believe a magazine could be ripped up into so many pieces by those small teeth? Did you know that to a puppy, a chair leg is edible and that tiny bits of dog saliva drenched wood are very difficult to vacuum up?

After we had finished, mom took me down to the mall for a milkshake. On the way, we picked up Gretel, and of course, Buddy came too.

While we go inside the milk bar, Buddy sits outside, tied up to a signpost. I feel bad about him being left out there, but we can see him through the shop window, so I know he is safe. Every second person stops and pats him. Buddy loves all the attention and rolls on his back for a tummy rub.

We had nearly finished our drinks, and Gretel said, "I'm definitely going to have to talk to my mom into getting a puppy."

I replied, "Yes, a dog is such fun. You'd be such a great dog, mommy!"

Gretel gave a slightly embarrassed smile, "I'm sure...but more importantly, have you seen how many cute boys have stopped to pat him?

That dog is a boy magnet!" Even mom laughed at that one.

We collect Buddy and go for a bit of a walk around the outside of the shops.

Mom had suggested Buddy might need to go to the toilet and told us to take him over to the grass footpath. That idea goes out the window when I see who is walking towards us.

A good day turns into a great day when we run into Mr. TDH and his mom, who have been shopping. Mr. TDH is very proud of his new shirt; he is even wearing it home with his old shirt in the shopping bag. I must admit it looks gorgeous, so clean and white.

While our moms talk, Mr. TDH fusses over Buddy as this was the first time he had met him. Buddy loves Mr. TDH and jumps up on him, licking his hand and any other part of his body he could reach. The feeling was obviously mutual! He licks Mr. TDH's face.

Gretel and I stand there smiling, and suddenly Gretel asks Mr. TDH, "Why is your shirt so wet?" Mr. TDH quickly puts Buddy down and gazes in horror at his new shirt, which has a huge wet patch with yellow liquid dripping onto his pants.

"I don't know what it is," said Mr. TDH, "but it feels warm." Suddenly it dawns on me; Buddy has weed on Mr. TDH in his excitement.

My face goes red as I apologize to Mr. TDH, "I'm so sorry, it's from Buddy."

The realization hits Mr. TDH. He rips off his shirt and holds it gingerly with two fingers outstretched from his body as far as his arms can reach. That got both mothers' attention fast. Gretel quickly explains what had happened; I was too busy apologizing still. Mr. TDH and his mom head home quickly to wash out his wet and smelly shirt while mom reprimands me for not taking Buddy to the grass footpath when she told me to.

Wednesday

I think Mr. TDH has finally forgiven me for the shirt incident, although I have avoided him since I am so embarrassed. Anyway, Gretel and I sat with him at lunch today, and he raved about how fantastic Buddy was, so I think all is forgiven.

Today I also developed a new interest in Robotics; I signed up for the School Robotics' Team. Gretel thinks that I only joined because Mr. TDH does it...but of course, that isn't true. I've watched several Star Wars movies and always like those two robot guys.

Mrs. Smith held the meeting about Robotics for the people that signed up, and it sounded cool. We will learn to program these little robots and send them through a course; there is even an inter-school competition.

Tonight, I'm studying up on the program booklet that Mrs. Smith gave us; I'm determined to do well.

Once we have mastered the basics of programming the Robots, Mrs. Smith said we would be able to take the robots home to practice on them.

The fact that Linda is also doing Robotics drives my ambition to be the best programmer at our school!

Friday

I love Robotics!!!!

No seriously! I really do...programming them to go where you want and doing what you tell them to do, is cool. Some kids would never join the Robotics program because they think it's just full of nerdy kids.

Well, it is kind of a nerd hangout...but the Nerdy kids have three things going for them: they're brilliant, they're friendly, and they've been kind and helpful to Mr. TDH and me. Thanks to our new friends we are getting good at programming. Although I must admit getting to work with Mr. TDH also makes Robotics very cool. Maybe one day I'll work at NASA, my office door will read Maddi Bull Programmer - Mars & Beyond.

Saturday

I organize to meet with Gretel at ten to take Buddy for a walk. We have decided to take him to the off-leash dog exercise park in town. It has a gate and is fully fenced, so we can let Buddy have a run around.

I walk Buddy over to Gretel's house, which is only two streets away. I do all the walking as Buddy decided after about 1 minute that he was too tired to walk anymore, so I carry him.

That, of course, leads to lots of people commenting on who's getting the exercise. One lady said to me, "I can see who the boss is."

Once I get to Gretel's house, I don't have to carry Buddy anymore. Gretel holds him instead.

When we reach the Dog Park and take Buddy's lead off, he suddenly is full of energy and starts running around sniffing all over the park.

I throw the ball I bought for Buddy to play with, he chases the ball frantically, but once he catches it, he won't let go of it. He brings it close to us and then runs away when we try and grab the ball to throw it again for him.

After many minutes of frantically chasing, Gretel and I collide and end up lying down on the grass. Buddy just moves to the shade of a nearby tree and watches us warily while he chews on his ball.

The fun starts when we decide it is time to go home. Buddy wouldn't come to us; he thought we were still playing the chasing game for the ball.

Our calls to Buddy went from nice, "Come here sweetie," to a screaming, "come here NOW!" Our attempts to catch him gave much amusement to the other dog park users; some were yelling advice...none of which was proving to be successful.

Eventually, we manage to trap Buddy in a corner and pounce on the rapidly tiring puppy. We quickly get the lead on him, but when we attempt to walk him home, he collapses on his stomach and refuses to move. Gretel and I take turns carrying him home. We arrive back at my place hot, tired, and sweaty.

Buddy, however, is rejuvenated and finds a squeaky toy and drops it at his feet. Hopefully, he looks at us with his big puppy eyes.

We both just groan and collapse onto the couch.

Sunday

Mom wakes me with her Mrs. Absolutely Positive loud voice and smile firmly fixed in place. "Let's take Buddy to the markets with us this morning," she said.

I sleepily drag myself out of bed and set about getting ready to go. It's then that I discover my favorite sandal, or should I say the many pieces of my favorite sandal. Tiny puppy bite-sized bits of my sandal scattered about the floor of my room.

Mom's response to my complaining about Buddy destroying my shoe is, "Well, you shouldn't have left your shoe lying on the floor," followed by the responsible pet owner lecture. Not the sympathy I was looking for.

The three of us, mom, dad, and I, head off to the markets held at the football fields. Usually, I'm not a keen market fan, but these markets are kind of cool with lots of yummy food stalls and interesting stuff.

Mom holds Buddy on his lead at the start, and of course, Buddy is amazingly well-behaved and cooperative. Buddy is the ultimate flirt! If a person looks at him, his tail goes into hyper-drive, and he gives out little whining noises. If they stop or talk to him, he drops down, rolls over onto his back, and hopes for a tummy rub.

As Gretel noticed on an earlier outing, Buddy is particularly liked by cute young boys, and he likes them back just as much. It's embarrassing because each of the cute boys' moms engages them in conversation and then introduces me to their sons.

How can that be bad, you ask, because each time she introduces me, she includes some interesting fact about me, one that isn't even true most times. For example, "What's your name? Josh, wow, what a lovely name. You look very fit; this is my daughter Maddi; she loves playing sport."

My list of incredible skills and abilities, according to Mom, includes dancing, singing, snowboarding, gymnastics, and probably going to the Olympics. When I complain to mom that she is embarrassing me, she laughs and assures me it is a parent's job to embarrass their child.

Mom then sends me off to get us some food with Buddy while she looks through some of the art stores.

I take Buddy's lead and head off. For the first few minutes, Buddy cooperates well. Then he starts trying to go in the opposite direction back to Mom. When that doesn't work, he promptly lies down.

I spent several minutes trying to coax him to get up and follow me. Fail! He lays there with his little tail wagging slowly.

Suddenly he leaps up, and his tail starts wagging faster. Yay, I think, at last. He bolts straight past me over to a group of young boys...not just any boys, but a group that has at least three of the boys Mom had talked to earlier.

"Hey," goes one of the boys, "it's Maddi and Buddy. She's a dancer, you know."

"No, Clint, she's a snowboarder," said another boy.

A third boy adds in, "I thought she was a gymnast."

"I guess I'm just multi-skilled," I stammer, not sure what to say, as my face goes bright red.

"Sorry, got to go," I said as I scoop up Buddy and rush off into the crowd.

I join a long line in front of a stall selling Mexican food. I notice the people right behind me were Mr. Skeil, a teacher from school, and his wife and small son, who must be about four years old. We exchange an awkward hello. You know, the type when students and teachers meet outside of school.

The line slowly shuffles forward. The smell of the food is making me hungry. Suddenly Mr. Skeil's son starts whimpering; the whimpering slowly grows louder until it is full-on crying.

I politely ignore it, as I don't want to embarrass the teacher over his inability to control his child's behavior.

Then an angry voice snaps over the crying, "Look what your dog has done!"

I look down to see the little boy's ice cream cone on the ground, and Buddy's face is covered in strawberry ice cream.

I pull Buddy away from the little boy and start to apologize. Mr. Skeil declines my offer to pay for another ice cream but gives me a version of the *being a responsible pet owner speech* focusing on keeping your dog under control.

I'm too embarrassed to rejoin the line and instead hurry back to Mom. I explain what happened. She bursts into loud laughter, which embarrasses me even more. Finally, she can control herself and then agrees to find Dad and take us all home.

Monday

Monday starts as a pretty normal Monday, although there was one awkward moment when I came face to face with Mr. Skeil in the hallway. However, he gave me a cheery, "Morning Maddi." Followed by, "How's your cute little pup going?" So lucky for me, there are no hard feelings there!

I'm feeling pretty excited today because my whole afternoon at school is devoted to the Robotics' group.

Miss Smith puts Mr. TDH and me with a kid called Charlie. Charlie is nice and patient with us, and we learned a lot from him.

Today we have been learning how to program the robot to go around a shape, like a square or a rectangle or circle. We have a felt mat on the floor with the different shapes on it that we try to program the robot to follow around. The rectangle and square shapes are easier because they are basically straight lines with a 90-degree turn.

Mrs. Smith throws down a bigger challenge. She lays a huge sheet of white paper down on the floor, and we have to connect a thick marker pen to our robot. We are still working in the same groups, and our group is given a red marker. We have to draw a circle, and an arrow, and Mrs. Smith gave Charlie an extra challenge of writing our two names Richard and Maddi. I bravely volunteered to control the robot to draw the circle (secretly hoping to show off a bit for Mr. TDH), leaving Mr. TDH the arrow.

Each group is given a small marked-out area of the sheet of white paper to work in. Mrs. Smith said it's okay if any of our tasks overlap as our area is quite small. We quickly knuckle down and start working out our programs.

Of course, Charlie was finished first, and his robot quickly and personally wrote our names, one on top of the other. Next, I did my circle, and Charlie had advised me to do semi-circles and join the top of each. It might have worked for him...but not for me. The top half of my semi-circles met in a rounded V shape, the bottom half in a stretched out point. My weird circle shape surrounds the two names that Charlie had written. As Mr. TDH starts his arrow, I realize my circle looked more like a heart shape. Mr. TDH's arrow goes straight between our two names, the arrow crossing my heart-shaped circle diagonally. As Mr. TDH's robot moves off the paper...this is what we had in front of us.

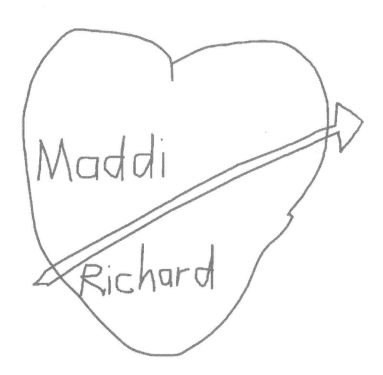

Both our faces blush bright red as Mrs. Smith gushes, "How romantic." That got everyone else's attention, and they all burst into laughter, except for Linda Douglas, who had a severe frown on her face.

Charlie looks at the paper and then back at us, "You guys are a lot better at Robotics than I had realized," says Charlie in awe. I'm pretty sure my face stayed red the whole way home, but I do have to admit, it was kind of nice.

At Robotics, Mrs. Smith introduces us to new equipment we'll get to use at the Interschool Robotics Tournament. The new gear is impressive; each robot now has a little inbuilt camera that can be connected to a laptop so you can watch where it is going on the laptop screen. There is also a little antenna that also connects to the laptop, so instructions to guide the robot's direction can be typed into the laptop and almost instantly relayed to the robot.

My Mars mission seems closer every day. We have a great time using the new gear and of course...Charlie is the best.

Mrs. Smith announces that the Robotics tournament will be held next Saturday at the local University. All our parents are invited, and Mrs. Cook will also attend.

Mrs. Smith then schedules several afternoon practices for us this week to get familiar with the new equipment.

Saturday

The morning of the robotic tournament arrives, and I wake up early. I had a very restless night's sleep. I'm feeling nervous about the tournament...worried I might mess up our team's chances.

However, I'm probably more nervous about the fact that Mum and Dad are giving Mr. TDH and his mom a lift out to the Uni, and I'll be arriving early, so the two moms will have plenty of time to talk.

I don't know about you, but when I get nervous, I have to make lots of visits to the toilet. So, by the time Mr. TDH and his mom arrive at our home, I've already made two quick trips to the bathroom. Mom noticed, and I had to assure her I was okay, just feeling nervous.

When our guests arrive, dad is outside mowing the lawn, so it's just the four of us sitting in the living room. Of course, Buddy was sitting next to me on the chair, as always. Mr. TDH sits next to Buddy and gives him plenty of cuddles, and we chat about the upcoming tournament.

I haven't told you yet, but Buddy has a very unpleasant habit of farting, and you wouldn't believe how bad he smells. They are always silent but deadly. So as luck would have it, Buddy let out a very smelly one. I pretend not to notice and hope no one else smells it.

Just as the smell from the first one clears, a second erupts that's even worse than the first fart. About the same time, my own stomach starts to gurgle, oh no, I'm going to need to go to the toilet soon, and everyone will think the earlier smells were from me.

Amazingly Buddy lets out a third fart. Mom says, "For goodness sakes, Maddi, go to the toilet!"

Then to our guests, she explains, "She's very nervous because of the tournament."

I feel the flush as my face goes bright red and start to say how it's not me but Buddy. However, at that moment, my bowel decides this is all too much, and I have to race to the toilet.

I finish my business, but I am too embarrassed to leave the toilet. Finally, I hear dad yell out, "Hurry up, Maddi! It's time to go."

I hurry out, wash my hands in the bathroom, and race to the car where everyone else is already sitting. I'm in the back with Mr. TDH's mom sitting between Mr. TDH and myself.

Mr. TDH leans forward and winks. He whispers, "Lucky that Buddy isn't coming too. I don't think the air conditioning would cope."

I grin back. Thank goodness Mr. TDH knows it wasn't me making the smells, and this is his subtle way to let me know. He is so lovely!

We arrive at the university and follow the signs to the robotic tournament rooms. There are lots of schools involved and heaps of kids heading along the pathways with us. We reach the entrance to the university building, and Mrs. Smith is waiting there to sign in our school team and assign us our name tags.

Once that is done, she instructs us to have a quick look around the tournament area and then report to room C, and the parents can take a seat in the tiered seating. The tournament room is enormous and has two levels. The second level is up a short flight of steps.

Our parents head off to the seating area as Mr. TDH and I go to find room C. Dad sees this as an excellent opportunity to embarrass me and booms out a loud, "Go Maddi!" as we walk away from them. Mr. TDH laughs as I put my hand over my name badge and urge him to hurry up.

We find room C and already have most of our team in there. Mrs. Cook stands at the front of the room and snaps at us to sit down quickly. She keeps checking her watch every few minutes. Mrs. Smith soon walks in with the last few kids, and Mrs. Cook gives her watch a final glance. "Are they all here yet?" she demands of Mrs. Smith. Mrs. Smith smiles and nods.

Then Mrs. Cook launches into a speech, but not quite the speech we were expecting. Basically, she emphasizes how we are representing the school and how important winning is as it will add prestige to our school. According to her...we should give a one hundred percent effort to ensure our school wins and not let Mrs. Cook down.

Mrs. Smith looks a little shocked by the tone of Mrs. Cook's speech. She announces, "Good luck, students. Mrs. Cook and I will enjoy watching you participate in such an exciting day."

Mrs. Cook butts in, "Unfortunately, I'm far too busy to stay and watch. Mrs. Smith, you can report to me on Monday morning." Then without another word, she quickly leaves the room.

Mrs. Smith looks embarrassed, "You'll compete with your usual team partners, and I've written the order of competition on these briefing sheets," she said.

She then continued, "Have fun, enjoy yourselves and make new friends. Winning isn't everything; I'm very proud of all of you."

Charlie, Mr. TDH, and I are the last team listed to compete for our school. Our school area is on the upper level, so we have a good view of not only our own competition table but also those tables below us. It's fun and exciting watching everyone else compete, especially as it's a really supportive atmosphere. Everyone is clapping and cheering each round winner during the events, regardless of which school it is.

As we head into the final rounds, three schools have been clearly dominant, Wolston Park, Greenfields Academy, an exclusive private school, and our school Harper Valley. In the middle of all the excitement, I feel a small knot of anxiety starting to grow in my stomach. Inside my head, I'm quietly hoping we don't end up with our team's performance deciding if our school wins or loses.

Of course, that's what happens. Going into the final round of competition, Wolston Park has fallen behind, so only Greenfields Academy and Harper Valley can win. As we prepare for our event, I can hear our teammates gathered on the other side of the table encouraging us. In amongst the cheers, I hear Linda Douglas shout, "At least they have Charlie and Richard." I try to ignore her, but it breaks my concentration, and I struggle to program my robot in the fifteen minutes allowed.

The final task is to program the robot to go through an obstacle course; it looks quite difficult. We can use the new equipment to adjust the robot's program as it passes through the course, but the robot will stop during the reprogramming. It's faster to get the programming right in the first place. The team with the fastest two finishes will win the round and the whole tournament for the team from their team of three.

The supervisors sound the start hooter, and the final round is on. Charlie's robot flies through the course, but he stops it just short of the finish line. He explains that as he hadn't crossed the finish line, he can still send his robot back to help if one of our robots gets stuck. A wise boy that Charlie, minutes later Mr. TDH's robot gets hooked up on the bridge's rail halfway through the course.

Charlie calls out, "I'll send my robot back and push you off the bridge!"

"No!" I reply, "I'm closer; I'll push him free with my robot." I quickly start typing my programming changes into my laptop. My robot stops as I program in the changes. I finish, hit enter, and my robot surges into life. It speeds through the course and reaches the bridge. It loses a bit of speed when entering the bridge, but finally, it reaches Mr. TDH's robot but only gives it a gentle nudge. Not only does Mr. TDH's robot not get knocked free, but my robot comes to a halt against Mr. TDH's robot.

I hit the keyboard again, and my new programming sees my robot back up and then accelerate towards Mr. TDH's robot at full speed. It slams into it with a thud, but Mr. TDH's Robot remains stuck. Frantically I key in a new instruction, and my robot backs up again but even further this time. Once again, it accelerates towards Mr. TDH's robot.

This time it hits the other robot so hard it gets airborne. I watch in horror as my robot flies off the table over the railing that separates the top level from the bottom level and lands on the Greenfield's table. Not just on their table but actually on top of one of their robots. It bounces off the other robot, taking the communication antenna with it. My robot lands upside down, its little wheels spinning uselessly.

The Greenfield Academy robot is damaged and out of control, just spinning around and around in the same place. I race down the steps to retrieve my robot; the audience sits in stunned silence. Except for my Dad, who booms out, "Way to go, Madonna!"

Meanwhile, Charlie sends back his robot to Mr. TDH's robot and starts to push it towards the finish line. I'm still apologizing to the other school's team as I reach across the table to pick up my robot. My shirt sleeve gets caught on one of the still-functioning Greenfield's robots just as my hand closes on my robot.

As I pull back my arm clutching my robot, the Greenfield robot snags on my arm, and it comes too. The robot's spinning wheels continue to run, and it gets even more caught up in my shirt. Now I've got two Greenfield's kids and a Greenfield's teacher frantically tugging at my shirt, trying to untangle their robot's wheels from my shirt.

Above all the noise, I hear the supervisor at our table yell out, "Harper Valley has completed the task!"

Then a *we've won* thought briefly flashes through my head before my ears are assaulted by the protests of the Greenfield's team. "They cheated!" "She broke our robot, and she stole our robot off our table!" are the most popular comments being yelled. I feel so embarrassed I want to disappear through the cracks in the floor.

The two supervisors meet on the stairs between the two levels and engage in a whispered conversation. It appears that one of them is upset, which is not a good sign.

By now, the Greenfield's teacher has finally untangled her team's robot from my shirt, and I slink back up the stairs to re-join my team. An excited Charlie and Mr. TDH both hug me. I realize then that they hadn't seen the destruction I had caused below on the Greenfield's team.

The supervisors finish their conversation, and the one from the Greenfield's table asks for everyone to be quiet. She then announces, "We have a winning team. As this is not robot wars (this is followed by a giggle from the audience), the Harper Valley team has interfered with the Greenfield's team's robots and is disqualified. I declare the Greenfield's team are the tournament champions."

The crowd claps enthusiastically. I quickly explain to Charlie and Mr. TDH what had happened at the Greenfield's table.

The three of us then go and congratulate the Greenfield's team. Mrs. Smith comes over to us with a big smile and gives us all a hug, with a, "Well done, team." She continues, "Without the bad luck, you would have finished ahead of them, even if Maddi's robot hadn't landed on their table. But it's fair that we are disqualified. After all, Maddi did single handily take out two-thirds of their team."

I think it's going to take a long time to live this one down. At least the car ride home was fun; we laughed all the way home with dad's entertaining description of what it looked like from the stands. Even I had to laugh when Dad referred to me as *destructo daughter*.

Wednesday

Costume ball, that's right, ball, not dance.

Mrs. Cook continues on her mission to destroy the lives of all her students.

Today she announced the school dance held at the end of each term would now become a costume ball instead.

We would all be taught how to "dance properly." We would learn the formal dances (old fashion dances), and no modern dancing would be allowed at all. Mr. Grant and some volunteer helpers will teach the dances in our normal PE lesson times.

That brings a groan from all the students who love sport, knowing Dodgeball would soon be replaced, and the only ball in the school gym would be the ball in ballroom dancing.

Thursday

Our first dance lesson, which is about to start, nervously our class herds together, everyone tries to avoid standing at the front.

Mr. Grant introduces the two volunteers standing beside him. The first is a lady with gray hair, Mrs. Velderham, and an older gentleman, also with completely gray hair, named Mr. Steiner. Mr. Grant informs us that both helpers are good friends of Mrs. Cook, and we should be grateful that they are giving their time to teach us.

I think Mr. Grant let us know they are Mrs. Cook's friends, so we don't say anything negative about the ballroom dance.

Mr. Grant tells us to grab a partner and form a circle on the floor. Nervously our class shuffles about. No one was keen to make the first move to choose a partner. I start to edge towards Mr. TDH when Linda Douglas sweeps in out of nowhere, grabs him by the hand, and drags him away.

Suddenly, a flurry of partner grabbing occurs, and before you know it, I'm left standing with the only other partnerless boy, Peter Kirk. Mr. Grant yells, "Hurry up, you two, join the circle; everyone is waiting for you."

We quickly shuffle into place, and then Mr. Steiner informs all the couples that first we will be doing the Pride of Erin. He tells us it is a dance dating back to 1911 in Britain.

Gretel is just behind me, and she whispers, "I think Mr. Steiner might have been there when they did the first dance."

I try to stifle a giggle, but it escapes anyway and attracts the evil eyes of Mr. Steiner.

"You! Why do you laugh? Do you think history is funny? The trouble with young people is that you have no respect for the past and your elders. Come here. You will be my dance partner as I demonstrate the dance," he snaps at me.

He then proceeds to try and demonstrate the dance with me, desperately trying to follow his instructions. I'm hopeless and just don't get it! But because I got in trouble for laughing earlier, at least no one else is going to laugh at me. Eventually, he gives up on me and orders me back to my partner with a parting comment, "Try not to kill your partner."

Mr. Steiner then partners with Mrs. Velderham to properly demonstrate the dance.

It's very complicated with a lot of hand-holding and forward and backward steps and twirling — a recipe for disaster when dealing with twenty-six clumsy students.

Fortunately, I was not the first to trip anyone over. That honor went to Sally Pearson, who stepped back when everyone else was going forward, tripping the girl behind her who went sprawling onto the floor.

You may have noted that I said *I wasn't the first to trip anyone over*...yes, that's right, I am the second kid to bring someone down.

When I twirl away from my partner, I tangle with Gretel, and we both end up on the floor.

Mr. Grant, perhaps worried by the mounting carnage, calls a halt to the dance session.

Saturday

Costume ball plus Mrs. Absolutely Positive equals potential public embarrassment for Maddi Bull.

Mom is being very enthusiastic about finding a costume for me for the ball. My feeble protests about simple, like a small plastic tiara on my head to make me a princess, are swept aside as Mum scans the Internet for 'something more dynamic' for her darling daughter. Her words, not mine.

Pictures flash before my eyes as Mom flicks from one costume to the next on her computer screen.

Suddenly, Mom stops on a robot costume; it's kind of cute, and as Mom says, it will go nicely with my new interest in robotics. The costume is fairly simple, cardboard boxes, one for the head and one for the body. Both are painted silver with bottle top lids glued on them as dials and buttons.

It looks a bit clunky and cumbersome, but the advantage of that is that I'll be able to get out of those dances and stay safely on the sidelines thinking of witty conversations to charm Mr. TDH.

Mom and I spend the rest of the day locating items to make the robot costume. It's fun! Mom and I are painting, cutting, and gluing all the bits together to create robot Maddi. By the end of the afternoon, when I try the boxes on, it's all coming together very nicely.

Mom says that on the night, she'll tape some aluminum foil around my arms and legs to give me that authentic robot look.

Thursday

Our second dance lesson starts the same way. First, we mill around, trying to avoid being at the front. I slowly push through the crowd aiming towards Mr. TDH. Today he's going to be my partner!

Mr. Grant stands in the middle of the floor, flanked by Mr. Steiner and Mrs. Velderham. They are wearing looks on their faces that say why we are wasting our skills here.

Mr. Grant calls out, "Grab a partner and form a circle quickly."

I burst through the few remaining kids between Mr. TDH and myself.

From the opposite side, I can see Linda Douglas approaching just as rapidly.

I dive for his hand and grab it, spinning him away from Linda.

Linda moves too fast to stop and plows into Mr. TDH's back, pushing him into me.

I have to grab him to stop us both from falling over.

Smiling triumphantly, I lead Mr. TDH out to the circle on the floor. Suddenly as we stand waiting for the instructions, the audacity of what I had just done hit me. I felt a rush of heat that started at my face and seemed to spread to my entire body.

Mrs. Velderham explains that today we will be doing a progressive barn dance, which means that the girl's line would step forward and change to a new partner at a certain point of the dance.

I can't believe it; all my effort to be Mr. TDH's partner will be for nothing. The music starts to play, and Mr. Stein calls out the dance instructions for us. As Mr. TDH takes my hand, the nerves hit me. I don't remember if I told you or not, but when I get nervous...I sweat. I get sweaty hands. So sweaty that I could probably solve the drought problems in the Sahara Desert.

So, no surprise, I feel the tiny beads of sweat start to trickle down my arms from my hands. I hope my sweat isn't trickling down Mr. TDH's arm as well. That would be rather gross for him. That thought makes my hands sweat even more, and now our hands pressing together are making squelching noises.

I'm sure Mr. TDH will never want to dance with me again. It's a relief when we get to the part when we change partners. I quickly wipe my hands on my shirt before I move on to my next partner.

The dancing goes on for what seems like forever. I'm slowly moving around the circle back towards Mr. TDH. I might get another turn with him yet. A few girls ahead of me, I see Linda Douglas. She moves up to become Mr. TDH's partner. She gives him a big smile as she becomes his partner, and to my annoyance, he returns it with a huge smile of his own. Just as we reach the part where the girl should move on, the music stops.

Mr. Grant is talking, but my attention is on Mr. TDH and Linda. Despite the dance having stopped, she is still holding his hand! Finally, I hear Mr. Grant's voice telling us to line up and get ready to move back to class. It's only then that Linda releases Mr. TDH's hand.

I feel my heart sink, and numbly I line up. Mr. TDH suddenly fills the empty space next to me in the line. He starts to say something to me, but I turn and walk away.

Friday

I arrived at school still in a grumpy mood from the Linda Douglas *hand-holding incident* yesterday. I'm talking to Gretel outside the classroom when Mr. TDH arrives and comes straight over to us. I restrict my replies to his attempts to make conversation to yes or no, then I drag Gretel away to go into class.

Gretel says, "You're being rude to Richard; it's not his fault if Linda didn't let go of his hand." Before we can continue this conversation, the teacher starts the lesson.

I notice Mr. TDH casting glances my way a few times during the morning. I also note that he seems to be having very little interaction with Linda.

Perhaps I have been a little bit unfair to the poor boy.

At lunchtime, when Mr. TDH asks if he can sit with Gretel and me, I respond with a friendlier yes, and a welcoming smile.

I'm such a kind and wonderful person. Mr. TDH seems very relieved that the frosty atmosphere has evaporated and talks to me non-stop during the break.

Happy days are here again!

Friday Night two weeks later

Tonight is the ball night, the last night I'll see Mr. TDH for three weeks. He's going away with his parents on a cruise, and he'll have no internet access so that we will be out of contact the whole time.

I'm super keen to get dressed in my costume and to get to the dance.

Mom asks, "While I get to the final bits of your costume ready, can you do the dishes." I go to the kitchen and start to wash the dishes, but I don't get too many done before starting to daydream about tonight.

From a distant place, I hear Mom calling my name, and I rush out of the kitchen (I know, a bit over-dramatic).

It takes a while to get dressed with Mom fussing over my costume, but at last, I'm dressed. I must say I do look outstandingly good. But unfortunately, another fifteen minutes is spent taking photos. You know what Moms are like with special occasion photos.

We have to have the photos of the robot, Dad with the robot, Mom with the robot, Buddy with the Robot, and the most time-consuming of all, the camera set on a timer to get Mom, Dad, Buddy, and the Robot.

Finally, we are done and head out to the car. The drive to the school for the ball is awkward. Oh no, not because of anything we said to each other but because my costume doesn't suit the car seat or seat belt.

After much maneuvering and a little bit of pushing and squashing, Dad fits me into the car.

We park and make our way to the school hall. At the entrance, Mrs. Cook stands to greet parents as they arrive with their children. She seems to be attempting a friendly smile, but it looks more like a zombie grimace. She looks me up and down as we enter the doorway. She doesn't recognize me, but when she looks at mom, a deep frown flits across her face.

"Mrs. Bull, an interesting choice of costume considering what happened at the robotics tournament," says Mrs. Cook.

Mom replies, "Not really when you consider how well the school team did to achieve second out of all those schools." With that, we swept past her and entered the main part of the hall.

Mr. Grant and the Costume Ball committee have done a marvelous job of decorating the hall. Combined with all the kids wandering about in their costumes, it looks fantastic. Maybe Mrs. Cook's idea of a costume ball wasn't so bad after all.

My parents sit down on some of the chairs set up around the walls of the hall. Meanwhile, I mingle with the envious children admiring my costume, not really. I'm a good robot, but there are some fantastic costumes on show tonight, from what I can see through the narrow slit cut in the box. As I catch sight of Linda Douglas in a princess costume attracting a lot of attention, I begin to question the wisdom of being a robot.

Then the dance music starts, and things deteriorate rapidly.

Mrs. Cook uses the PA system to make an announcement. "Welcome to our first ever Costume Ball, and thank you to everyone here for making such a wonderful effort with their costumes. I'm so happy to see so many supportive parents here today. I hope everyone enjoys the night, and I am so proud to be the leader of this amazing school."

Tricked you! That is what she should have said. Instead, she yelled into the microphone, "All students are to find a partner for the first dance, do it quietly and hurry up!"

I'm 12, and I could do a better job! I look over at my mother, and she is smirking and shaking her head. Dad is laughing out loud! Oh, how I wish I could laugh as well...

I start to move to the side because, as per my plan, my costume is too cumbersome to dance in.

Mr. Grant suddenly appears in front of my limited vision. "Come on, Maddi, Mrs. Cook said that all students have to participate in the dance," he states firmly.

"But Mr. Grant, I'm clumsy enough in normal clothes, let alone dressed in cardboard boxes with a very limited view of the hall," I reply.

He brushes off my objections and tells me, "Maddi, go and find a partner. I saw a nice lego-man over there who would make a perfect partner for you."

I stroll onto the dance floor and find lego-man, moving as awkwardly as I was.

We survive the first dance amazingly well, no one ends up on the floor, and we only have a few minor collisions.

The next dance is not so successful. It's the progressive barn dance. The trouble is when we change partners, my side vision is so restricted I have trouble seeing the boy, let alone the boy's hand, which I'm meant to grab.

The first few changes of partners are merely embarrassing; the last one is a disaster of epic proportions.

As I move onto Peter Kirk as my partner, I try to grab his hand but miss altogether. Panicking slightly, I take another more forceful swipe, miss his hand but definitely didn't miss his head. I feel my hand slammed into his face and my little finger slide into his eye.

He yells out, "My eye!" and clutches both hands to his face.

We both stop, and the rest of the dancers pile into us. The dance line grinds to a halt, and someone stops the music.

Above the noise of the kids and parents, the loud, clear voice of Peter Kirk can be heard, "She got my eye, she hit me in the face and nearly tore out my eye!"

The surrounding noise drowns out my apologies, so I try and pat him on the shoulder but unfortunately, with my stiff arms, I misjudge and hit him on the back of his head.

By now, Mr. Grant is on the scene and applies his usual calm manner to settle things down. He looks at Peter's eye and pronounces it will be okay, and leads Peter away to apply some ice.

Mrs. Cook announces, "Quickly, students to your places; the dance must go on."

With no partner, I quietly escape to a corner vowing to myself that I won't dance again. Standing alone, I watch the others dance. Mr. TDH certainly catches my eye dressed as a very dashing Robin Hood. I feel a pang of jealousy as I see Princess Linda Douglas move on to become Mr. TDH's dance partner.

I have to admit, she looks beautiful as a princess. I feel slightly better when she moves on to the next boy, but I notice she keeps looking back over her shoulder at Mr. TDH.

Finally, that dance ends, and I successfully remain hidden in the corner for the following three dances.

Then Mrs. Cook makes us all parade around the hall in a single file so that everyone can see our costumes. Then she announces the boy and girl winners of the best costumes. Of course, Mr. TDH and I are announced as the winners and have to waltz around in the middle of all the other students to the thunderous applause of all the parents and teachers.

No, not really, only kidding, again! After all, this is a Maddi story, not a fairy-tale. Some other kids, much cooler than Mr. TDH and robot girl, won and got a voucher for an ice cream from the canteen.

Mrs. Cook picks up the microphone again. Everyone has the same reaction...I can see a lot of eye-rolling. "Students, attention students, this will be the last dance. I'm sure you are as keen to go home as I am. So, hurry up and find a partner."

Across the other side of the hall, I see Linda Douglas race over to Mr. TDH. They have a quick conversation, and I see Mr. TDH shake his head. Leaving Linda standing there, he starts walking in my direction. As he gets closer, he gives me a big smile. Bowing towards me, he asks, "May I have the pleasure of this dance, Maddi?"

Of course, I answer, "Yes," and we join the circle on the floor.

Despite having Mr. TDH as my partner...my dancing is still no better. But it's fun dancing with him, and I enjoy it despite my clumsiness.

Finally, the dance ends, and we stand facing each other awkwardly. I wish Mr. TDH a great holiday just as I hear his dad telling him to hurry up.

Mr. TDH pulls out a red envelope from his pants pocket; I can see my name written on it.

Nervously he stammers, "I got you a card, open it when you get home," and hands it to me. My arms are so restricted I can't reach far enough to put it in my pocket. Realizing this, Mr. TDH takes it back and slips it into the ventilation slot that Dad had cut into the back of my head box.

His father calls him again, and he smiles at me as he says, "See you later," and hurries off.

On the trip home, my heart is racing at a million miles an hour. I wonder what Mr. TDH has written on the card. The drive seems to last forever, but finally, we arrive home. Once we go into the house, I race off to my room to take off my costume and read Mr. TDH's card.

Buddy follows me in and starts trying to rip the foil off my legs. My puppy helper slows me down, but at last, I'm transformed back to Maddi with my robot costume lying on the floor.

I've just picked up the box to get out the card when Mom storms into the room. "Get yourself into the kitchen, young lady, and finish the dishes I asked you to do before we went to the ball," she doesn't sound happy.

"Just a minute mom, I just need to do something first," I replied.

A stern "Now!" and a pointed finger towards the kitchen is answer enough that my card will have to wait. I dump the box in my hand onto the floor and head off to the kitchen.

After four hours, actually, it was only ten minutes but did seem a lot longer, the dishes are finally done. I race off to my room to read the card. As soon as I walk into my room, the devastation is obvious. Sitting amid the mess is Buddy, still chewing on the only intact box. Scattered amongst the chewed up cardboard, I can see wet and slobbery bits of the red envelope. The red envelope which contained the card from Mr. TDH.

I start gathering the bits of the envelope and discover some of them still contain pieces of the card. I stockpile them into two piles on my student desk, one pile for the envelope and one pile for the card. When I appear to have collected all the bits, I start to try and re-assemble the card.

Matching up wet chewed-up pieces of the card is more challenging than your average jigsaw puzzle. Slowly but surely, the card starts to take shape. The front of the card is a write-off, the picture seems to have been of flowers, but the dog dribble has made the ink run, so it's too hard to make out the picture.

The inside is in slightly better condition, and I can clearly read:

Dear Maddi, thanks for always making me laugh and being a great partner at robotics. Would you be

Be what? My brain races with possibilities, but the most popular choice with my brain cells, is **my girlfriend**.

The bottom part of the card was missing. Frantically, I burrow through the mess on the floor but find nothing more of the card. Mr. TDH is away for three weeks! Can I last that long not knowing what he was asking me?

Meanwhile, Buddy, who is still chewing on cardboard while lying on the floor, makes a strange burp noise. As I turn my attention to him, he stands up and makes a few heaving movements. Then a pile of vomit spews from his mouth onto the bedroom floor. Clearly sticking up in the middle of the vomit is a piece of the red envelope. YUCK! Do I really want to put my hands in a pile of dog vomit?

While I consider my next course of action, Buddy, obviously feeling better, starts to lick the edge of the vomit pile. Realizing he is about to re-eat the mess, I grab him and put him outside my room, and close the door.

Do you know that dog vomit smells terrible? You probably do, but I bet you didn't know it also feels horrible when it is all warm and slimy. Yes, I put my fingers into the vomit, searching for any other fragments of card and envelope.

Please don't go all squeamish on me; you know you would have done it too.

The only bit I could find was the bit I initially saw sticking out of the mess.

I carefully open and flatten it out to discover another fragment of the card. This could be it, the message revealed.

I pull out the card only to discover the writing it once contained…is now a totally unreadable mess of smudged ink.

Disaster! My room smells of dog vomit; my fingers are dripping dog vomit, and I can't find out what Mr. TDH wrote for three weeks.

AGGGGHHHHHHHHHHHHH!

Poor Maddi!
I hope you loved this Almost Cool Girl book!!!
Can you do me a HUGE favor and leave a review?
Thank you so much!
Bill
(Secretly, I'm an almost cool Dad.)

We really appreciate and love
our readers! You are amazing!
If you loved this book, we would really
appreciate it if you could leave a review
on Amazon.

You can subscribe to our website
www.bestsellingbooksforkids.com
so we can notify you as soon as
we release a new book.

Please 👍 Katrina's Facebook page
https://www.facebook.com/katrinaauthor
and follow Katrina on Instagram
@katrinakahler

Some other books you may enjoy...
Not just for boys!!!

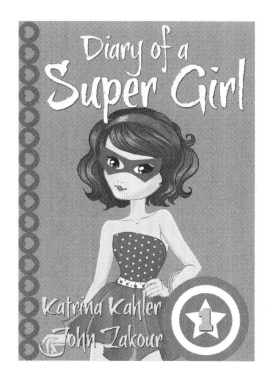

BE SURE TO CHECK OUT
OUR BEST SELLING
COLORING BOOKS, JOURNALS & DIARIES.

KIDS ALL OVER THE WORLD
LOVE THESE BOOKS!

Printed in Great Britain
by Amazon